MW01247234

PATRIOTS

A Story of Bunker Hill

by Gregory T. Edgar

Illustrated by Todd L. Gerlander

Copyright © 2000 Gregory T. Edgar

BluewaterPress edition 2009

Cover Photograph and Design by Ron Godbey

Note to teachers: A Teacher Guide is available for *Patriots*. The author is also available to do school presentations. For a free copy of the Teacher Guide, or his brochure on school presentations, e-mail him at: Gregory_Edgar@ Hotmail.com.

Other books by the author include the following:

Juvenile Novel:

Gone to Meet the British (the sequel to *Patriots*, this book is also published by BluewaterPress)

Adult Non-fiction:

"Liberty or Death!" The Northern Campaigns in the American Revolutionary War

Campaign of 1776, The Road to Trenton

Reluctant Break with Britain, From

Stamp Act to Bunker Hill

The Philadelphia Campaign 1777-1778

All rights reserved. No part of this book shall be reproduced, stored in a retrieval system, or transmitted by any means without the written permission of the publisher.

International Standard Book Number 13: 978-1-60452-028-6
International Standard Book Number 10: 1-60452-028-0

Library of Congress Control Number: 2009933044

BluewaterPress LLC
52 Tuscan Way, Ste 202-309
Saint Augustine, FL 32092
http://bluewaterpress.com

Information regarding the puchase of this book may be found online at
http://bluewaterpress.com/patriots

MAIN CHARACTERS

Ebenezer ("Eben") Dunham A 13 year-old boy living in Boston in 1775.

Lydia Dunham — Eben's mother.

Major John Pitcairn — An officer in the British army. He is staying at the Dunham house, against their wishes.

Will Pitcairn — The major's 16 year-old son, a Regular (Redcoat), who is also staying at the house, and acting as his father's servant.

Barnabus Dunham — Eben's father, who escaped from Boston the night after the Lexington-Concord raid. He has joined his cousin's company in the Patriot army.

Lieutenant Joseph Reed — Barnabus's cousin, an officer in the Patriot army.

Danforth ("Danny") Reed — Joseph's son, a 14 year-old fifer in the Patriot army.

"When all is said and done, a battlefield is no fun."

-From *"The Little Sergeant,"* a song of the American Revolution.

PREFACE

Hello out there, whoever you are. My name's George Robert Twelve Hewes. My friend Mr. Edgar, the author of this here book, asked me to help him out. Said he knew I was once a Son of Liberty in Boston in the old days. That's true; I was a true Patriot who fought for liberty – what we called "the Cause" back in 1775.

Mr. Edgar said it was only proper that someone like me write a "Preface" to this here book. Well, I don't know what a Preface is, but I told him I could try to write a few words down. Maybe explain to you folks what was going on back then. How it led up to the first big battle of the Revolution – the Battle of Bunker Hill, which is what his story's about. So here goes.

First off, before any of you folks get confused; let me set the record straight about the name of this here battle. Don't be fooled! The Battle of Bunker Hill really took place on Breed's Hill, not Bunker Hill.

You see, we Patriots were supposed to build the fort on top of Bunker Hill. But instead, we built it on the next hill we came to – Breed's Hill – which, of course, should have been the name for the battle. Problem was, some chowderhead back at camp – who wasn't even at the battle that day! – wrote a report about the battle. *Said it took place on Bunker Hill, when everyone knows it took place on Breed's.*

Hmmh! What a chowderhead! Oh well, enough about that. Let me get on with what I'm supposed to tell you folks.

It was 1775, the year before we declared our independence. So we were still the colonies, you know, not states yet. Each of us was a citizen of the British Empire, just like the people in mother England itself way across the ocean.

But the British government for many years had not been treating us right. For one thing, they kept thinking up new laws that said we had to pay some kind of new tax on this thing, or that thing. It seemed like every year they thought up a new tax to lay on us. It was very annoying!

Well, we weren't about to let someone way across the ocean tell us what to do, no sirrah! Those of us who loved liberty and called ourselves "Patriots" or "Sons of Liberty" decided to do some thinking of our own. We thought up clever ways to protest the new taxes. When I say "protest" what I mean is we'd get together and do something to let the British know how we felt about these new taxes.

I remember one night, whooee! Why, we dumped a whole shipful of British tea leaves right into Boston Harbor! Boy, the fishes drank tea that night. We all knew it was wrong, of course. But we had to do it to make sure no one could buy the tea and pay the hated tea tax.

Hundreds of us Sons of Liberty dressed up that night as Mohawk Indians – to disguise ourselves, you know. We painted our faces, grabbed our tomahawks, and headed for the tea ship, yelling, "Mohawks, grab your axes, and pay no taxes!"

As you might expect, the British government didn't like that.

To make us behave and pay the taxes, they sent an army over here to Boston. Well, we didn't buckle under, no sirrah! Instead, we prepared to defend ourselves, and fight for our rights.

We started collecting bullets, and muskets and cannons, and of course, gunpowder to fire them off. We stored it all in a town outside of Boston. Sure enough, the British army learned about it from their spies, and planned a raid. They marched out of Boston, real sneaky like, in the middle of the night. They wanted to march to Lexington and Concord, to find and destroy the stuff we'd collected, so we couldn't use it against them.

That night, my friend over in Boston – Paul Revere – was keeping his eye on the Regulars. Oh, I suppose I should explain why we called the British soldiers "Regulars." It was because soldiering was their regular job, not like us Patriots who only did soldiering when we had to.

As I was saying, Paul saw the Regulars about to march out of Boston on their secret night raid. Paul just knew he had to do something to warn the Patriots. He decided to sneak out of Boston himself – which was a mighty dangerous thing for Paul to do with all those British Regulars everywhere.

But Paul made it. Rowed across the Charles River, he did. Borrowed a horse from a Son of Liberty on the other side. Rode that horse as fast as he could, to spread the alarm. What a night! Paul woke up Patriots in all the towns he went through. As he rode by, he shouted, "The Regulars are out! The Regulars are out tonight!"

Many years later, some poet who wasn't even there that night wrote a famous poem about the midnight ride of Paul Revere. Maybe you heard of it. Ever since then, people think that Paul shouted, "The British are coming! The British are coming!"

Well, don't you believe that nonsense. Who you gonna believe

– a trustworthy Son of Liberty and personal friend of Paul's – or some chowderhead who wasn't even there?

Grabbing their muskets, Patriots came running from all directions. We shot at the Regulars all day long, as they marched back to Boston. Of course, we fought the way the Indians had taught us to when we first came here. You know, by taking cover behind trees and stone walls. The Regulars' bright red coats made easy targets for us to shoot at.

Oh, those British Regulars didn't like that. Said we didn't fight fair, and they would get even, first chance they could. That chance would come a few weeks later, just across the river from Boston, over on Breed's Hill. You know, the Battle of Bunker Hill.

Well, there you are. Time for my friend, Mr. Edgar, to tell you his story. So long for now.

Your most humble and obedient servant,
George Robert Twelve Hewes, Son of Liberty

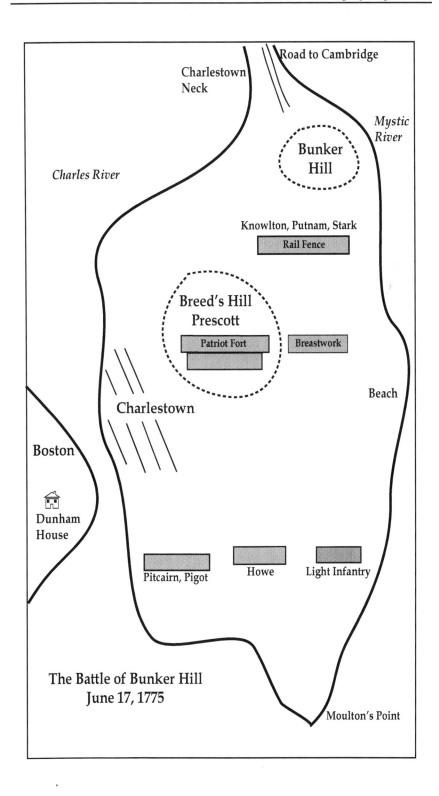

The Battle of Bunker Hill
June 17, 1775

CHAPTER ONE

Boston, June 16, 1775

Mrs. Lydia Dunham was alone this afternoon in her house in Boston. As she often did, she was worrying about her husband. She had not seen him or heard from him in nearly two months now – not since this awful war started, back in April.

On that evening of April 19th a very tired British army came marching back from Lexington and Concord. The Regulars, or "Redcoats," had marched all the way to Concord, 18 miles. They wanted to find and destroy weapons they'd heard Americans were collecting to prepare for war. But the country people – at least those who called themselves "Patriots" – had stood up to the British soldiers – first, at Lexington, then later that day at Concord. And the Patriots fought them all day, along the road leading back to Boston.

That evening, two months ago, her husband watched the returning Redcoats. He told her, "The war has come, Lydia. I must do my part. Now that it's started, tonight's my last chance to leave Boston and join the Patriot army. I must do my part for the Cause."

Barnabus kissed Lydia and their son Ebenezer goodbye and left. Thinking back to that night, Lydia wondered if her Barnabus was safe. *Perhaps,* she thought, *he managed to reach the Patriot lines ... or perhaps the British shot him.* She didn't know.

Barnabus was not her only worry. Her son, though only thirteen, had set his mind on going with his father. Barnabus had to be sharp with Ebenezer that night. Ebenezer must stay behind to look after Mother and the house, keep them safe from the British and "Tories." Tories were Americans who favored the British, and didn't like the Patriots.

Since then, Ebenezer, or "Eben" as he preferred to be called, spent most of his time with other angry boys in town. Often, they would look for a Redcoat or two to bother. Just last week, Eben came home with a cut on his ear and a black eye after their latest fistfight with a British Regular.

Lydia constantly had to remind Eben to be polite to Major John Pitcairn and to his son, Will, who was serving in the British army as the major's servant. They had moved into the Dunham home last month. The people of Boston had to make room for British officers in their homes, even if they didn't want to. It was the law – another one of those new British laws the Patriots hated.

Lydia Dunham's thoughts were suddenly interrupted by a commotion downstairs. It was her son arriving home after what must have been a long run, because he was puffing. He shut the door loudly and stumbled up the stairs to the one room they now were forced to share.

"Eben, what's wrong?" his mother asked. Instead of answering, Eben brushed past her and pulled the curtain shut. He flopped down on his bed, burying his face in the pillow. Ever since Major Pitcairn and his son had moved in, Lydia and

Eben had to share one of the two upstairs bedrooms. Major Pitcairn's son used the other upstairs bedroom, and the major slept in the larger one downstairs.

A bedspread draped over a rope served as a curtain to divide the room in two. Lydia waited on one side of the curtain, listening to Eben sobbing into his pillow on the other side.

After he stopped sobbing, she asked softly, "Eben ... do you want to talk about it?"

"No!" came the muffled reply.

But Eben could no longer hold it in. He lifted his head from the pillow and talked rapidly. "I wish I was a man! I'd show them, every one of them! I'd have a gun, and be with Father, and make all those lobsterbacks go back where they came from. We didn't ask them to come over here. Why don't they just go back to England and leave us be!"

"Eben. Please come out and talk to me." After a few moments Eben pulled back the curtain and stood in front of his mother. His breathing had slowed to normal now. But he was still upset, so he walked back and forth, head down, in front of her.

"Oh, Eben! What happened to your face?"

He stopped and put the fingers of one hand gently on his cheek to feel it. It hurt. He walked to the mirror to see for himself. Eben mumbled, "I got hit by a fish."

"Speak up, child, I can not hear you."

"I said, 'I got hit by a fish!'"

Moving carefully, his mother put her arms around Eben.

"Oh, Ebenezer, child. Tell me what happened this time. Were you fighting again?" She wished her son would try harder to stay out of trouble.

"No, I was not fighting. I was down to Clark's Wharf. I

saw Hezekiah Smythe, the fishmonger, there. He was selling fish to the British. Can you believe that, Mother? And Father always said Smythe was such a good Patriot. Some of our people were asking him to sell or barter them some fish, you know. He acted real uppity, and looked down his nose at them. 'Sorry, only for His Majesty's officers,' he said. Well, I couldn't help myself, I called him a Tory."

"So he hit you with a fish?"

"Ye- yes, but not right then." Eben frowned. "First, we sort of had an argument."

"I see," Lydia said, trying to be patient. "Go on, I want to know the rest. Don't leave anything out."

With a frown, he agreed. "Okay, Mother." He let out a long sigh. "Let's see ... after I called him a Tory, he came closer to me and acted strange, almost friendly, you know. But some of the things he said didn't make sense."

Trying to remember, Eben started walking back and forth again, slower now. He used his hands as he talked. Lydia sat down in the rocker and listened to her son.

"I remember Smythe said something like this: 'Well now, if it ain't that Dunham lad. Now ain't he the spitting image of his old man Barnabus. And, for that matter, his old man's cousin Joseph. Ain't that something now. Why, Barnabus and Joseph look like twins sometimes, you know, like two peas in a pod in a Cambridge garden.'"

"He flew off the handle then..."

Eben looked down at his mother to see her reaction to such a strange thing to say to a body. She made no expression, though, so he continued his story.

"Then I told him that not only was he a Tory but he's blind as a bat, too, if he thinks my father and Joseph Reed look alike. He flew off the handle then, Mother. Before I could finish my sentence, he reached out and smacked the side of my face with a big, stinking fish. It knocked me down. I yelled back at him, 'If my father was here, he'd give you a pounding.'

"So then he leaned forward and put his fish breath face real close to mine. And he said, 'I ain't afraid of Barnabus and Joseph together.' Then he repeated it: 'I ain't afraid of the two of them, Barnabus and Joseph together, so there! Go home and tell your mama that, boy, and see what she says.'

"Isn't that strange, Mother, to talk like that? Mother, I think Hezekiah Smythe is teched in the head. And – and then he started hitting me with the fish again, saying, 'Git! Go on home, and tell your mama!' Then he laughed. They were all laughing at me.

"Especially that nasty Will Pitcairn. He was there, too. Buying fish for the major, he was. I wish they'd both move out of our house. They don't belong in a Patriot house. They should live with Tories, or go back to England where they belong."

Lydia Dunham didn't say anything. She was smiling now, a tear forming beneath one of her closed eyes. For a moment, she held her hands clasped together in prayer. Then, suddenly, she jumped up, saying, "Praise the Lord! Your father is safe!" She grabbed Eben's arms and danced around him in a little circle. He shook himself free and looked at her in wonder, thinking now his mother was acting crazy, too.

Eyes wide, she answered his look. "Don't you see, Eben? Hezekiah –" She caught herself and put a finger to her lips. She walked over to the door to shut it. When she came back she continued in a soft voice. "Hezekiah's not really a Tory. No, he's just pretending to be one – he's a messenger! Oh, yes. Think about what he said, Eben."

He was still puzzled, so she explained. "Hezekiah must have seen your father with his cousin Joseph. Why else would he keep on saying, 'Barnabus and Joseph together'? He's probably working for the good doctor, Joseph Warren, the Patriot leader. Because Hezekiah sells fish to the British, they let him come in and out of Boston. He gathers information and carries messages back and forth to Doctor Warren and the other Patriot leaders. That's my guess. Now, what did he say about peas?"

"Huh? Oh ... that Barnabus and Joseph ... were 'like two peas in a pod ... in a Cambridge garden.' That's it. That's what he said, I'm pretty sure."

"Like two peas in a pod ... in a Cambridge garden," she repeated slowly.

Now Eben figured out the rest. "That must mean Father and cousin Barnabus are together, and in Cambridge! I've heard tell the Patriots have their main camp there. Father is safe! He made it through the British lines!"

CHAPTER TWO

Early that evening

L ydia and Eben ate dinner in the kitchen, as usual. Only Major Pitcairn and his guests were allowed to use the dining room. Eben and his mother did not speak to each other during dinner, because Will Pitcairn was in and out of the kitchen, waiting on his father and his dinner guests.

After dinner, Lydia waited until they were alone before whispering, "Eben, you must not mention what happened today to anyone. If word gets out that Hezekiah is carrying messages, it won't be long before the British hear of it and arrest him. I think they hang spies."

"But Mother, how can I keep such news from my friends. We can trust –"

"No! Absolutely not! We can't trust anyone with this. Not a soul. We simply can't take chances with other people's lives, Eben."

After a while, she said, "I'm going to retire early tonight. The news about your father has lifted such worries off my mind that I feel very tired. You can go out for a while, but be sure to be in before dark."

Eben knew he must be home before dark because, ever since the war started, the British general had placed a sunset curfew upon the town. Any American caught on Boston's streets after dark could be arrested as a spy.

Eben started down the hill to look for his friends. But his mind was not on them. Again and again, his thoughts returned to Hezekiah Smythe. It puzzled him.

How, he thought, *can a dirty fishmonger be a spy? Spies are supposed to be well dressed gentlemen who walk with a gold-tipped cane tucked under one arm. And the arm of a beautiful lady of quality in the other. Hezekiah is a fishmonger, a big ugly brute dressed in rags. And he smells like the dead fish he sells. If he can be a spy, anyone can!*

The thought inspired him. He remembered that the major was entertaining other officers at dinner tonight. Eben turned around and returned by a roundabout route. He approached the house from the rear, so no one in the dining room would see him.

Because of the hot and humid mid-June weather, Major Pitcairn had the dining room windows open to catch any sea breezes that might come in. So Eben crept up to the house and squatted down under one of the open windows to see if he could hear the officers talking. He guessed that by now they had finished dinner and were drinking wine and smoking their pipes.

Eben's heart was beating so loudly he thought surely they could hear it and would nab him at any second. He had a bad feeling that one of them would suddenly feel the need for a breath of fresh air and stick his head out the window. The

Eben squatted down under one of the open windows...

words his mother had said came back to him now: "I think they hang spies." Eben pictured himself with his hands tied behind his back and someone placing a rope around his neck. His stomach began to feel queasy.

Eben's legs were starting to shake from crouching so long. He decided he could hear just as well sitting on the ground. He felt very hot. His sweat made his shirt stick to his chest and back. *Lord,* he thought, *it's hot down here out of the breeze.*

At first, Eben could not make out what they were saying inside, only a phrase now and then. The birds chirping in the trees, and his own breathing and heartbeat, combined to make it difficult to hear. Eben closed his eyes and blocked out all sounds but the voices.

"I say, it's about time we broke out of this town and taught those Yankees a lesson. Eh, John?"

"Yes, I dare say you're right, Basil." Eben knew that was Major John Pitcairn's voice. "My men have been asking for the chance ever since that nasty Concord business in April."

"It's been bloody humiliating, I must say," the one that Pitcairn had called Basil said. "Stuck here in this God-forsaken stinkhole of a town, shut up by a rabble of peasants and shopkeepers. E gad!"

"By George! We'll give it to them." This was a third voice. "They won't be able to hide behind trees and stone fences this time. We'll take along plenty of artillery to force them out in the open. Then we'll see if they can fight like Englishmen. We'll strike at their main camp in Cambridge. Those we don't kill will run away back to their farms. We'll end this silly rebellion once and for all!"

"Hear, hear!"

"Hear, hear!"

"Yes. Gentlemen, I believe a toast is in order." Eben heard a chair scraping on the wood floor. *That must be Major Pitcairn standing up.* Eben heard someone walk a few steps before stopping. Next, he heard a faint bubbling sound, a few more steps, and again the bubbling sound. The steps were light. Eben guessed it was Will Pitcairn, the major's son and servant. *Will must be going around the table refilling their glasses with wine.*

"To the eighteenth, and victory!" Major Pitcairn declared.

"Victory!" his guests all responded together.

Drops of sweat, pouring down Eben's scalp and forehead, stung his eyes. He wiped his eyes, thinking about what he just heard. *The eighteenth. The British must be planning to attack our Patriot camp on June 18. Let's see ... what day is today? – June, June 16. Ohhh ...*

Eben's heart was racing faster than ever now, and he suddenly felt a strong urge to visit the outhouse. *Errh! Not now!* He wanted badly to stay here and listen to more of their talk about their secret plans for an attack. But Eben knew from the urgent feelings in his bowels that his pants would soon be full if he waited much longer. He had not felt like this since that time last winter when he had the grippe.

Eben crawled a ways at first. Once he was beyond their earshot, he quickly stood up and ran to the outhouse in the backyard. As fast as he could, he closed the door and pulled down his knee britches and unders, just in time. "Ahhhh! Thank you Lord, that was a close one!"

Eben's breathing and heartbeat were still racing. He

thought about this sudden call of nature and figured out what must have caused it. Hearing those British officers talk about attacking the Patriot camp had made him awful scared for his father. Eben laughed to think that his brain and his other end could be connected like that!

While Eben sat on the seat, he thought about all that he had just heard. He mulled it over in his mind. *Father is in danger and must be warned. But he told me to stay home.* Eben remembered his father's serious face and his words that night two months ago: "Protect Mother and the house from the British and Tories."

Hmm ... Stay home and protect Mother. Stay home and protect Mother. But Father is the one in danger!

Eben could not decide what to do. And it was becoming nasty inside the outhouse. There was no breeze to take away the heat, humidity and smell. He needed fresh air to think clearly. He grabbed another scrap of newspaper to wipe himself once more, and threw it down the hole. Then he pulled up his unders and knee britches, opened the outhouse door, and stepped out.

Outside, the air seemed much cooler and the sea breeze felt good on his forehead. "Let's see," he thought out loud. "Protect Mother from the British and Tories. Well, no Tories have bothered us yet, and they are not likely to with a British officer living in our house. And Major Pitcairn has always acted like a gentleman to Mother, and never threatened her. I'm sure he won't let any other Redcoat bother her. So what good am I doing by staying home? I should be with Father, doing my part for the Cause.

"Even cousin Danforth signed up. True, he's only a fifer,

but he's there doing his part. Maybe he could teach me how to play a fife. Or a drum! A musket would be better. They shouldn't make you be sixteen to sign up as a musketman!"

Seeing a stone on the ground, Eben kicked it as hard as he could with his right shoe. It stubbed his toe, but made such a loud bang when it hit the outhouse door that the pain was worth it.

"And what about Father! He could be killed, along with a lot of other good Patriots, too, if I don't do something. That settles it. I've *got* to warn Father. Perhaps he'll be so pleased he'll let me stay in the army for a while. I'll go tonight."

CHAPTER THREE

Later that night

Though the hour was late, Major John Pitcairn was still up. He was writing at the desk in the first floor bedroom. His friend in London, England, would be glad to hear from him. The major carefully stroked his quill pen across the paper. After every few words, the quill ran dry and he dipped it again in the inkwell. He wrote:

> The rebels – they call themselves "Patriots" – are not true soldiers. Because they are many, they think they are an army. But we know what they really are – farmers and shopkeepers playing at war. They put muskets in their hands and fool themselves into believing they can fight our trained army. They will soon find out how weak they are when they have to come face to face with our Regulars.

"Major Pitcairn! Major Pitcairn!" It was Lydia Dunham's voice calling him. Her feet coming down the stairs sounded loud and hurried. Now she stood in the open doorway looking very frightened. The major quickly returned the quill to the inkstand and stood up to answer her. "Goodness, Mistress Dunham! What is it?"

"Oh, major. Sir, I beg your forgiveness for disturbing you at this late hour. It's my son, Ebenezer – he's run away! You know how the British sentries are with anyone they find on the streets at night – I'm afraid they will shoot him on sight. Oh, my God! Help me, please!"

"Whoa. Slow down madam. What makes you think your son has run away?"

"Well, I woke up and, from habit, I looked over to see if Ebenezer was sleeping soundly. He was not there! He's gone!"

She's obviously upset, Pitcairn thought. Her hands were clenched in tight fists, and she was taking quick, deep breaths. *I must calm her down.*

Walking around the desk and towards her, he said in a soothing voice, "Please, sit down." He took her arm and led her to the easy chair just inside the door. "There. What makes you so sure, madam, your son has run away. Perhaps he woke up to go to the outhouse. Surely that's it. I can go out back and check, if you wish."

"No." She stood up. "You do not understand. ... Here. He left me this note." She opened her tightly clenched fist and handed him a small piece of paper. The major held it up to the candle and read it aloud.

Dearest Mother,

Please forgive me but I must do my dooty. I am leaving to join father in the Patriot armie. Please do not worry. I shall be very careful not to be caught by the Redcoats. I will send word to you that I am safe as soon as I can.

Your affeckshunet son,

Ebenezer Dunham

"Major ... can you find him? Before the sentries do? I'm afraid they will shoot first, and ask questions later. He's just a boy, sir!"

Major Pitcairn thought a moment before answering. He spoke calmly and slowly. "Madam, we do not know in what direction your son went. He could have tried to leave Boston by land or by sea." *God knows*, he thought, *the boy will not likely succeed either way*. "Searching for him in the dark of night would be like – well, like searching for a needle in a haystack.

"And do you really think, madam, that your son would come out of his hiding place if he heard *me* call out his name in the darkness? He might think I came to punish him. Think about it, madam."

Lydia looked the major in the eye. At first, she had to work to control her shaky voice, but it grew stronger as she went on.

"Major Pitcairn, the day – the day you moved into my house – against my wishes – you assured me, on your honor, that you would protect us as long as you stayed here. Well, now sir, one of us is in danger. I am appealing to your honor as a gentleman to keep your word and help me."

He frowned and walked away from her for a few steps with his head down, thinking. Stopping, he turned to face her and slowly threw open his arms. "It appears, Mistress Dunham, that I have no choice in the matter, do I? I will go and search for the boy. But I shall *not* be out on this wild goose chase all night! I shall not."

The major walked with long, loud steps to the staircase and yelled up to his son. "Will! Will, get dressed and fetch our mounts from the stable. We have to go out tonight."

A few moments later, Will Pitcairn came running down the stairs. "What – what is it, Father?"

"Well, son, it appears the Dunham lad is missing. You and I are going to search for him and bring him home, before the sentries find him first."

"I don't want to –"

"Enough! We'll have none of that talk, Will. Now, go fetch our mounts, like I told you to." Will frowned, rushed past his father, and slammed the front door behind him.

While he waited for his son to bring the horses, Major Pitcairn thought about Ebenezer's choices. *The boy probably knows better than to try swimming across the Charles River. And all boats he might steal have been collected by our guards by now. So he must be going by land. There's only one way to go – he'll try to slip past the guards at the Town Gates on Boston Neck.*

Major Pitcairn decided not to waste any time. He would ride directly for the Neck and talk to the officer on duty there. He would advise the man to be on the lookout for a boy about Ebenezer's age. Of course, he would have to offer the man a reward for bringing the boy back.

Major Pitcairn was adjusting his wig in front of the mirror when Will returned. "Our horses are saddled and ready, Father. I'll wait for you outside."

"Good, good. Thank you, son."

Before leaving, he tried to put Lydia Dunham's mind at ease. Placing his hands on the outside of her shoulders, he forced a smile and looked in her eyes. "If your son doesn't turn up tonight, he will most likely return in the morning – ashamed and embarrassed – to ask your forgiveness."

After walking to the door, the major turned to add, "Good evening, madam. Try to get some sleep if you can." He was gone before she could reply.

CHAPTER FOUR

Major Pitcairn and his son rode down Snow Street and headed for Treamont, which ran nearly the length of town. As he was passing the grassy Common, he shook his head and laughed to himself – he could not believe what he was doing. "Look at me now, Will. I've let a rebel woman talk me into a midnight search for a snot-nosed rebel brat. What a world, this America!"

Seeing his father in a lighter mood, Will decided to speak freely. "Father, if I may say so, sir, I think this is a fool's errand. We both know that the Dunhams are rebels. As a rebel, he deserves whatever happens to him."

"I know, son, I know. But I did give the lady my word that I'd protect her family as long as we stay in her house. A gentleman always keeps his word. Remember that, Will."

Will wasn't sure he agreed. He asked, "Even if that gentleman gives his word to a rebel?"

"Yes, son. A gentleman *must* keep his word. It's a matter of honor."

Leaving Treamont, they turned onto Orange, the only street on Boston Neck. The narrow "neck" of land connected the peninsula of Boston to the mainland. They slowed their mounts to a walk when they saw lights up ahead. That would be the lanterns of the guardhouse next to the Town Gates.

"Father, did you hear that? ... There it goes again! It sounds like someone screaming out in pain."

Each scream came a few seconds after the one before it. Major Pitcairn had spent many years in the British army. So he knew such sounds could mean only one thing – some poor soldier was being whipped.

But the screams didn't sound like a man's voice. Quickly he spurred his horse. Seeing this, Will did the same. They galloped the rest of the way, the major in the lead, shouting as he went. "Guard! Guard! Halt that!"

Major Pitcairn reined in his horse, handed the reins to Will, and jumped down. "Who's in charge here?" he demanded.

A big, mean looking, and slightly drunk Redcoat stepped out of the darkness and angrily answered, "Who wants to know?"

"Major Pitcairn, Marines. State your name and rank, soldier, if you are responsible for this post. I demand to know what goes on here. Who is being whipped, and why? ... Speak up, man, or you'll find yourself at the other end of that cat-o'-nine-tails!"

The man quickly lost his bad attitude and saluted the major.

"Sergeant Thomas Towns, Ninth Regiment of Foot, sir! Begging your pardon, sir, we caught this young rebel trying to slip past our post here. We hailed him, but he wouldn't stop. We had to run him down. Gave us a bit of a struggle, too. One of my men said he'd seen the lad before. There's a gang of saucy boys been bothering our off-duty soldiers just this past week. Well, sir, here's one rebel that won't be walking the streets for a good while, we made sure of that!"

The sergeant was surprised to notice an angry look come over the major's face. So he quickly continued in a different tone. "But, we – we went easy on him, sir – we surely did. Didn't even use the whip on his back – no, no sir! We used a switch, you see. Took it from that bush over there. We laid it on gently, on the soles of his feet. That's just what we did."

Major Pitcairn frowned. "You sound mighty pleased with yourself, sergeant. I have a mind to report you for using too much force. In the future, if a rebel tries to get past you, just stop him and hold him. Leave it to an officer to decide if a flogging is needed." After letting out a loud sigh, Pitcairn said, "Show me the boy."

Before he followed the sergeant, Pitcairn spoke to his son. "Perhaps, Will, I should have this sergeant reported. ... Nah, likely nothing would come of it. After all, the boy had it coming, if the sergeant was right about bothering our men in town. The Dunham lad needs to be taught a lesson." Will nodded his head heartily in agreement.

Major Pitcairn found the boy had passed out from the pain. And yes, indeed, it was Ebenezer Dunham, just as he feared it might be. The boy had been tied with rope to the barrel of a cannon. That way, his feet, stripped of their shoes and stockings, hung out past the open muzzle of the cannon. Both feet were bleeding from the soles and insteps.

In the dim light of the lanterns, Pitcairn could not tell how bad the damage was. But he had seen cases like this before. Unless an infection set in, the boy would survive.

Pitcairn thought, *He will be limited to bed rest for a few days. After that, he'll have a period of hobbling around the house before he can cause any more mischief.*

He won't be able to climb the stairs for a while. Likely he and his mother will have to use my bedroom, and I'll have to move upstairs. A minor matter, to be sure, but bloody unseemly for one of His Majesty's officers to have to move out of the best room in the house. Hmmh! These Americans will be the death of me yet.

Major Pitcairn turned to mount his horse. "Sergeant, untie the boy and bring him to me. And be careful with him. Don't let his feet touch the ground. You can give his shoes and stockings to my son to carry."

"Yes, sir. Thank you, sir," the sergeant answered, glad to be rid of this troublesome officer. The big sergeant quickly turned to his men. "Well, you heard the man! Move!"

The two sentries were surprised that this major would take an interest in a rebel boy. They looked at each other a moment, then shrugged and followed their sergeant's orders. Together, they lifted Eben up so he could sit, even though not awake, in front of Major Pitcairn.

Putting one arm around Eben's chest, the major pulled gently on the reins to turn the horse around. They headed slowly back to town.

"I know it's very late, Will, but I'm going to stop on the way and have the doctor take a look at his feet."

"But –" Will started to object.

"Hush!" His father was in no mood for arguments. "You go along now, son. Tell Mistress Dunham I'll be home with her son, soon. Go on."

* * * * *

After cleaning and bandaging Eben's bloodied feet, the doctor used smelling salts to revive him. The doctor needed Eben to be awake so he could swallow a dose of laudanum for his pain. Waking up made Eben aware of the pain in his feet. He began to moan, and to swear again at the British army, just as he'd been doing before he passed out.

Major Pitcairn waited in silence. He was surprised to find himself worried for the boy. He insisted that the doctor sell him the rest of the bottle of laudanum. He could give it to Eben's mother to use when she thought her son needed another dose. The major also made the doctor promise to visit the Dunham house the next day.

Major Pitcairn carried Eben out and swung him up onto the horse. Standing on the ground and looking up at Eben, he spoke firmly. "Stay awake, and keep hold of the saddle's pommel. Don't fall off."

Major Pitcairn walked the rest of the way to the Dunham house, leading the horse by the reins. Every now and then, he looked back to see if Eben was still awake enough to stay in the saddle. When they arrived, Will was waiting for them on the front step. "How is Mistress Dunham, Will?"

"She's inside, Father. A bit upset, I suppose." Will took the horse away, while his father carried Eben into the house.

Lydia Dunham was much relieved to see her son alive. She wept, and hugged him so long in front of the major it embarrassed Eben. She was very, very angry when the major told her about the whipping. She surprised Eben by boldly speaking out against the British army, right to the major's face.

Eben was glad to hear his mother finally express the same feelings he had about the Redcoats. But he worried she would go too far. Knowing the major was a proud man, Eben wondered how the major could stand to listen to such abuse from his mother. Now Eben recalled how concerned for him the major had been at the doctor's house, and during the ride home.

He could not remember, though, the major arriving on the scene. The last thing Eben could recall before Major Pitcairn carried him out of the doctor's house was being whipped while strapped to a cannon barrel. *I must have passed out, and the major must have rescued me from those evil men.* Eben was confused. He knew he should hate all Redcoats. But, when he looked at the major now, he admired the man.

Major Pitcairn poured a drink for Eben's mother and tried to talk her into sitting down. Mrs. Dunham would neither drink nor sit down, though, until she gave her son a second dose of the laudanum. She knew that Eben needed rest and, because of the pain, would not be able to sleep without the medicine.

Eben wished the major would go somewhere and leave the two of them alone. He wanted to explain to his mother why he had tried to leave Boston. *I must tell her everything now –*

How I listened in through the open window during the major's dinner party. About the secret British plan to attack the Patriots' camp in Cambridge. Father is in danger, and must be warned. Surely, Mother will ... understand I ... had to warn Father. I ... need ... to tell ... her ...

It would have to wait until tomorrow. The laudanum was working fast. Eben could not keep his eyes open. Sleep came upon him and took away his pain.

CHAPTER FIVE

Bunker Hill, that same night

E ben had failed to warn his father and the other Patriots. But the Patriots had plenty of other spies inside Boston. So the Patriot leaders found out about the British plans. They decided to not wait for the British to attack them at their camp in Cambridge, which was on flat ground. Instead, they would build a fort atop one of the Charlestown hills. The British would have a hard time in the hot sun marching up a hill to attack the Patriot fort.

At the same time that Lydia Dunham was asking Major Pitcairn to search for her missing son, 1,000 Patriots were secretly marching up Bunker Hill. The work party that was sent there to build a fort that night included Lydia's husband Barnabus, Eben's father.

With Barnabus was his cousin Lieutenant Joseph Reed, and Reed's 14 year-old son Danforth, who was a fifer. He liked to be called "Danny." When they reached the top of Bunker Hill and stopped there to rest, Danny looked up at his father to whisper a question.

"Father, is this here ground we're on Bunker Hill? How can we tell in the dark? Maybe it's that other hill, yonder."

"I know what you mean, son," Joseph Reed whispered back. "Dark it is. But I think they said the first hill we come to would be the one we're supposed to fortify."

Barnabus Dunham agreed with his cousin. "Your father's right, Danny, this hill is the one named after farmer Bunker. In fact, if it was daylight now, you could look this way," he added pointing into the darkness, "Straight past Breed's Hill there and see my house. It's on a little hill called Copp's Hill over in Boston, on the other side of the Charles River."

His own mention of his home made Barnabus think of Lydia and Ebenezer. *They must be asleep now. Lord, keep them safe. I wonder if they received that message I gave to Hezekiah Smythe.*

Danny, too, pointed into the darkness. "Then those lights, yonder, they'd be Boston?"

"Yes, they would, Danny," Barnabus answered.

"And those over there," Danny asked again, moving his hand to the left this time, "why are they flickering like that?"

"Ah," Barnabus nodded, "those would be British ships, floating at anchor. They're not actually flickering, they just appear to be. That's because the ships are bobbing up and down with the waves."

"Are they war ships?"

Barnabus could see that the boy was a little nervous. "Yes, they probably are war ships. But don't you worry none about them, Danny. We're far away from them."

Their private talk atop Bunker Hill came to an end when the captain came walking swiftly towards them. "We've got new orders. We're all moving forward to the next hill. Everybody up!"

"Captain," Joseph Reed objected, "this *here* is Bunker Hill! That one's Breed's."

"I know, lieutenant, but General Israel Putnam spoke to the other officers a few minutes ago. He told them, 'To heck with those orders, let's build the fort on Breed's Hill, yonder. It's closer to Boston, so the British will have to try to force us off the hill. If they don't, our cannons will be close enough to blast them to bits, make them sail back to England.'

"Now, get the men moving. Remember, no talking. And keep those spades and shovels from clanging into each other. We don't want to be discovered before we have a chance to use them."

They marched off Bunker Hill and down into the swale between the two hills, then up the north slope of Breed's Hill. It was slightly lower than Bunker Hill. But it was at least 500 yards closer to Boston, and that's what mattered most. Breed's Hill was so close it would force the British into action.

Soon dirt was flying through the air. Since most of the Patriots were farmers, they were used to using shovels and spades to dig up stumps. So the fort's walls quickly began to take shape. The night was warm and humid. After a while, some of the diggers stopped to take off their hats and coats as they worked up a sweat.

CHAPTER SIX

Breed's Hill, dawn the next morning

They worked in shifts. Half would dig, while the other half kept watch. Colonel William Prescott, a Massachusetts officer in charge at the fort, gave strict orders: No one was to shut his eyes. Prescott did not want to be surprised by the British.

By five o'clock in the morning, the fort was about half done. The sections that were complete had a wall about six feet above the outside ditch. It would not be easy for the British to come over these walls. The strongest wall faced Boston. The rear wall, facing Bunker Hill, had a narrow opening where the Patriots could go in and out.

In the dim light of first dawn, the diggers became aware of their danger. One by one, they stopped work to look around. Danny looked down at the harbor less than a mile away. He saw British war ships floating at anchor. Danny thought they looked ready for a battle. He counted them. "One, two, three, four, five, six, seven, eight!"

He heard a nearby man mutter under his breath, "We were all brought here to be killed. This hill's too close to those ships' big guns. Bunker Hill was safer."

* * * * *

As the Patriots gazed down at those British war ships, someone was staring back at them.

Hardly believing his eyes, a sailor aboard the ship *Lively* saw something that had not been there the evening before. "A fort! Impossible!" He ran to wake the captain of the ship. The captain grabbed a spyglass, and hurried out of his cabin to peer up at the hill.

Yes, it was true. "Rebels!" he muttered. He shouted orders to his crew. "Swing this ship around! Point our guns at that hill!" Quickly, the gunners were wakened and ran to their cannons. "Fire! Fire at will!"

* * * * *

Barnabus, Joseph and Danny were on digging duty inside the fort when they heard the first boom. It sounded like thunder. Danny looked up at the sky. Not a cloud in sight. "Take cover!" someone shouted. Startled, Danny crouched behind the wall. Those outside threw down their tools and jumped into the ditch.

Danny peeked over the wall. He saw smoke drifting over the water in front of one of the British war ships. Suddenly, a 24-pound cannon ball landed with a thud below the fort and bounded up the hill towards a group of men still standing.

They quickly joined their wiser comrades and jumped into the ditch.

Other balls started landing, but they, too, fell short. They bounded and skipped for a while, before rolling harmlessly away to the left or right down one of the sides of the hill. Some rolled straight up the hill and came to a stop just short of the fort, before rolling straight back down into Charlestown's upper streets.

One man laughed at them all for showing fear. "They can't even reach us!" he boasted. "If you want to play hide and seek, go ahead. As for me, I'm gonna fetch me a souvenir."

Curious, Danny watched the man as he waited for the next one. Before long, Danny and the man both spotted a flash of bright yellow fire from the side of the ship. The flash was followed a moment later by a loud boom. A perfectly round hollow ring of smoke left the muzzle of the cannon's barrel and drifted through the air, over the sea.

Danny saw the man look up, searching the sky. He must have caught sight of the cannon ball in flight, because he took off running. The man kept his head up, following the ball's downward path, as he gave chase along the side of the hill.

"Fool, leave it be!" someone shouted at him. But the man paid no attention; he wanted that cannon ball. The ball plowed a furrow in the sod when it first landed, then took a couple bounces as the man closed in. The heavy ball was nearly past him and about to start rolling down the side of the hill. The man wouldn't let it get past him.

Quickly, he stuck out a foot to slow the ball down. The ball hit his leg just above the ankle. Everyone on that side of the fort heard his shin bone crack. It reminded Danny of the sound a tough chunk of oak makes when he splits it in half with an ax. Back and forth, the man rolled on the ground, screaming in pain.

Danny dropped his shovel and ran over to see. Dozens of men and boys crowded around, staring down at the injured man. They didn't notice, behind them, a few Patriots taking this chance to slip away, to desert. The deserters ran towards Bunker Hill and the safety of the mainland beyond it.

Colonel Prescott wasted no time removing the man from the work site. He assigned four men the task of finding two stout poles and a blanket to make a stretcher. He told them, "Carry the fool back to camp, then return here with a barrel of water." As soon as they started off, several others tagged along to "help."

As Danny watched them go, he thought to himself, *They won't return. They're cowards. Not like me and Father, and cousin Barnabus.* Danny couldn't help feeling, though, that maybe the deserters were the smart ones.

The colonel addressed the crowd. "Let this be a lesson to all of you. No good ever comes from a man leaving his post. Now, let's all get back to work. ... C'mon, now. Everyone back to your posts."

They obeyed his orders, many of them muttering as they walked back to the fort.

CHAPTER SEVEN

Boston, that same morning

"Father," Will Pitcairn asked, as they walked towards Boston's Long Wharf. "I think, as soon as we bring our army across the river, the Yankee rebels will all run away. They won't stay to fight. We can then march against their main camp at Cambridge, as planned. Do you agree, Father?"

The major smiled and looked down at his son. "Yes, Will, they'll probably run away, once they see us coming at them. But, I'm hoping they stay in their little fort and give us a fight."

"Huh? –"

"That's right, Will. We need them to stay and fight, so we can gain a victory today. We need to beat them badly. Take prisoner all who don't die in the fighting. Kill or capture the whole lot of them. Not let them escape back to their camp."

He explained why. "Then the rest of that 'rabble in arms' they pretend to call an army will lose heart. They'll go home to their farms, disgusted for letting themselves be duped into rebellion by rebels like Sam Adams and Joseph Warren. In a few days, word will spread south to the other colonies, and this rebellion will quickly fizzle out."

They reached the wharf. Will looked with pride on the crowd of more than 2,000 brightly uniformed Regulars. In just a few hours they would make quite a show marching up Breed's Hill. *How can those Yankees possibly have the courage to stay in their little fort and fight against us?*

Will Pitcairn could hardly wait to cross over the water and get on with it. This would be his first battle, and he could almost taste victory already.

CHAPTER EIGHT

Boston, that same morning

Very slowly, Lydia and Eben made their way up the narrow stairway from the second floor. It led up to the "cupola," which was a tiny room on the roof. Eben had heard the cannons from the British war ships and guessed there would be a battle very soon. He wanted to be in a good spot to watch it. There was no better view in all of Boston than the cupola on their very own roof.

In the stairway, Lydia tried hard to lift Eben as much as she could, so he wouldn't have to put his weight on his injured feet. Eben did his part by grabbing hold of the railing and pulling himself upward. By now he felt like fainting because of the pain in his feet. But he wanted to continue. "Just a few more steps, Mother. We can make it."

They struggled up another step. Lydia saw her son wince from the pain once again, and it made her angry.

"Ebenezer!" she scolded him. "This foolishness of yours is tempting the Lord! You will have a fever and be sick in bed for weeks. I thought climbing to the second floor was unwise, but now this, all the way up to the cupola. Just look at your feet, boy! See, they've started bleeding again. Your bandages are soaked!"

She let out a sigh of disgust, and wiped her brow. They were both drenched in sweat.

"You're a stubborn boy, Ebenezer Dunham. Just like your father is a stubborn man, leaving us alone so he can go off and play war." She started to weep bitter tears of anger and fear.

"Please don't cry, Mother. Father is with Cousin Joseph. We know that now. They are probably still in camp, in Cambridge. And even if he *is* on that hill, yonder, I'm sure he's safe enough behind those walls."

Eben wished he could sound more convincing. But he, too, was worried about his father. And angry at not knowing whether his father was one of those Patriots in danger, over on Breed's Hill.

"I'm ready now, Mother. Let's finish these last few steps." Eben winced in pain with each step as he pulled himself along by his left hand on the railing. His right hand hugged his mother's right shoulder to balance himself, while she tried to lift his body with both hands around his chest. Finally, they reached the last step. There was one chair in the little room.

"Here Eben, sit in this chair." She helped him ease into it. "I'll be back in a minute with the spyglass. And a stool for your feet." Lydia Dunham went back down the stairs, muttering to herself about the foolish ways of men and boys.

Wow! The view was perfect! It was a clear day, the morning fog already burned off by the hot sun. The view made Eben's struggle up the stairs worthwhile. He could easily see the Patriot fort atop Breed's Hill.

He guessed it was complete now, because the Patriots were no longer working on it. They were outside, building a "breastwork," a wall about breast high. It ran from the fort's front wall part way down the far side of the hill, towards the Mystic River.

Lydia returned, put Eben's bandaged feet on the stool, and handed him the spyglass. Eben used it to look more closely at the breastwork outside the fort. "Mother, look. See that extra wall they're building? I bet that's to protect against an attack from that side. Do you think so?"

Lydia did not answer. She had a worried look on her face as she looked out the side window at something directly below them on their own Copp's Hill. Eben noticed her. "What – what is it, Mother? What are you looking at?"

"The artillery park right below us. There are two British officers in very fancy uniforms. And soldiers standing by their cannons."

"I want to see. Yes, please Mother, help me over."

A few moments later, they looked down together. "They look like generals," Eben said excitedly.

They saw a rider approach, rein in his horse, and lean down to hand a piece of paper to one of the generals. After reading it, the general said something to the messenger and he rode away. The two generals talked to each other, probably about the message, Eben guessed.

"Let's open the window. I want to see if I can hear them."

The window had not been opened in several months, but they managed to finally pry it loose and lift it up.

Eben stuck his head out the window to see if he could hear the two generals. Lydia, though, was not interested in listening to other people's private talk. Instead, she walked around the inside of the cupola, taking in the view in each direction. There was a window on each of the four sides.

Eben strained his ears, but he could not hear the generals. They were too far away. Soon, though, he figured out what the message must have been. He heard one of the generals call over an artillery officer who'd been inspecting the guns' sightings. A few moments later, the artillery officer shouted to his men. Both Eben and Lydia clearly heard him shout, "Commence firing! Fire at will!"

BOOM! ... BOOM! ... BOOM! the cannon sounds crashed through the air. It was as if Lydia and Eben were in the middle of a loud thunderstorm. Startled, Eben quickly pulled his head inside, bumping the top of it – "Oww!" – on the bottom of the window.

They both put their hands over their ears. The white smoke from the cannons drifted towards them. Coughing, they struggled once again with the window, this time to shut it. Eben wondered how the soldiers working the big guns could stand the noise. He thought, *Perhaps they are all deaf.*

Lydia shouted at him, "I better go see if anything needs to be taken off the shelves downstairs."

Eben sat in the chair and watched a cannon ball fly through the air towards the Patriots on Breed's Hill. "Duck!" he yelled, though he knew they couldn't hear him. Eben cheered when he saw the ball miss its target.

After several minutes, Eben's mother returned carrying a lit candle. She blew out the candle, then handed Eben a still

"Commence firing! Fire at will!"

warm ball of candle wax. "Here. Put this in your ears, and join me in prayer. ... Dear Lord, protect our husband and father Barnabus today from whatever evil comes his way. ... And, and guide him in Your work, Lord. Help him to do what he must. Amen."

Eben added his own request. "And please, Lord, keep Major Pitcairn safe, too."

CHAPTER NINE

Breed's Hill, that same morning

D anny took a break for a minute. He was tired of digging. He watched Colonel Prescott walk around the outside of the fort to inspect it. The walls looked ready, rising six feet above the outside ditch. And, on the inside, they were just high enough for someone to stand on a firing step and place his musket barrel over the wall.

Danny saw Prescott, walking outside the fort, stop to talk to a man working hard on the far side of the ditch. Of all the workers, this man was closest to the British war ships.

"Good work, Asa Pollard," Colonel Prescott said cheerily.

Looking up, Asa smiled and answered, "Oh, thank you, colonel. We'll be ready for them when they come, you'll see." Colonel Prescott started to walk away to the right.

"Take cover! Down, colonel! Get down!" The colonel threw himself flat on the ground. A distant hissing sound quickly became a screeching roar as it passed directly over the colonel's head with a rush of air. *Thwack!*

Danny heard the sickening sound, like a pumpkin being smashed. He looked over and saw that the backs of Colonel Prescott's legs were splattered with blood. Looking a few yards to the left of the colonel, Danny saw on the ground the bloody remains of Asa Pollard – now a headless corpse. Danny quickly bent over and vomited on the ground.

The shocking news spread quickly. Men and boys left their posts and came running over to stare at the headless body. Grown men were crying like young children, others were vomiting as Danny had done.

Many of the Patriots had seen enough. They dropped their tools and started running. They wouldn't stop until they crossed Charlestown Neck and reached camp. One man, as he ran away, shouted to those who stayed behind, "Save yourselves! We are sold!"

CHAPTER TEN

Breed's Hill, early that afternoon

The hard labor of digging the outside trench and building the walls was finished. The Patriots inside the fort could rest now. Their officers would wake them up as soon as the Redcoats began their advance.

Inside the fort, Joseph Reed and Barnabus Dunham sat on the firing step. They rested with their backs against the wall. Their eyes were closed beneath the wide brims of their floppy felt hats, pulled down to shield their faces from the bright sun.

A few of the others were praying, preparing for the worst. But most of the Patriots were like Joseph and Barnabus, simply resting. Some were calm. Some were fidgety, and nervous about the coming battle. Many were thinking about the chances they'd had earlier to run away.

Most of them, like Danny Reed, had never been in a battle before. Never faced enemy fire – or, as the saying went, never "smelled powder." And never been forced to kill another man. Danny was thinking about that now, and worrying about it. *The Bible says, 'Thou shalt not kill.' But the Old Testament has all those stories about the Israelites having battles.* It was hard to decide what was right.

Danny hadn't heard anyone talking for a while now. He knew that, if they were like him, their throats were dry and hoarse from the dust and having nothing to drink. He looked at the ground outside the fort. There he saw the remains of the last two water barrels. Their wooden staves had been shattered by a British cannon ball. The big puddle they'd made was gone now. The sun was so hot.

Unlike his father and Barnabus, Danny couldn't sleep. So he stood on the firing step and looked out at the enemy. He was dead tired, and his body ached for rest. But he did not want to sleep now and risk missing something. In all his fourteen years, he had never been involved in anything this exciting before.

Earlier, Danny had watched dozens of flatboats slowly make their way over from Boston. Each boat had been crammed full with forty Regulars. Their scarlet red coats had stood out against the deep blue of the sea.

Sailors, wearing white, had rowed them across. They'd dipped their oars into the water all together, and pulled them back all together. Slowly but steadily, the flatboats made their way across the water.

The cargo those boats carried was 2,000 Regulars – the Redcoats. They, too, would soon work together, slowly but steadily advancing up Breed's Hill. When they reached the fort, they would force Danny and the other Patriots to fight to the death or run away. Danny had thought about all these things as he'd watched them cross the water.

Now they had landed. They were all spread out on the grass, just 500 yards below the fort. They had been there for some time. He wondered, *Why don't they attack us?*

He wondered, *Why don't they attack us?*

CHAPTER ELEVEN

The shoreline, below Breed's Hill

The British officer in charge of the attack was William Howe, their best general. He had landed at Moulton's Point in the first boat so he could lead his army. While he waited for the rest to cross over, he gave the troops permission to rest. The Regulars gladly laid down their muskets, and slipped their knapsacks and haversacks from their backs. However, no one dared take off his thick, woolen coat. Many took out part of their rations and ate their mid-day meal.

The Regulars were hot already, and they had not even started their march up the hill yet. They cursed this awful North American weather. It almost never was this hot back in England. The sky held no clouds to block the harsh sun straight overhead.

As Danny Reed stared down at them, General Howe and General Pigot were relaxing. They sat on the grass under a shade tree. They sipped from wine glasses and discussed the rebel defenses, and their own plan of attack.

The two generals stopped when they heard harsh voices. Yells and curses came from the direction of Charlestown. The voices were coming closer. Howe and Pigot handed their wine glasses to their servants, and stood up.

They saw Major John Pitcairn and some of his Marines very roughly leading five British soldiers towards them. Will Pitcairn helped hold one of the men. Will's father halted the party in front of the generals. Major Pitcairn saluted them by taking off his cap and lowering it with a sweeping motion to his thigh.

"General Howe. General Pigot. Please forgive this intrusion. Some of my Marines were searching Charlestown for rebel snipers. They found these five scoundrels hiding in a house."

Two of the accused men were red-faced and hot from struggling with their captors. They scowled and glared at Pitcairn. The other three looked meek, and as pale as ghosts. They nervously glanced about at the hundreds of soldiers staring at them in silence. There was a hush as everyone strained to hear what General Howe would say.

"Major Pitcairn, thank you for bringing these traitors to my attention. And to that of every brave and honest soldier here. As soldiers of His Majesty's army, they know very well the penalty for desertion."

Without pausing, General Howe pointed at the two scowlers. "Hang these two. Send the other three back to their officers. We can't afford to lose five soldiers today."

The crowd was silent no more. Those in front, who had heard the general, whispered his words back to those behind them. It was passed on back from there. Pretty soon, the whole army seemed to be whispering at once. No Regular would dare desert after seeing this.

The two scowlers, at first, protested that it was unfair to be singled out. That failing, they started cursing General Howe, the British army, and even the king and queen.

Turning to General Pigot, General Howe said, "Come, my general, let us look at our enemy once more." They picked up their spyglasses off the ground and walked away from the tree. An officer called for two ropes.

When the two generals returned, they saw the entire army standing at attention. All except two soldiers who were now hanging limply from the tree.

Will Pitcairn had been thrilled to be one of the Marines who had caught the deserters in Charlestown. Will was proud to be a British Regular, and even prouder to be a Marine led by his own father. He was not nervous about facing the Yankees. His father had trained him well.

But Will had just watched in horror as the two scowlers were hung. He blamed himself. *If we had not found those men in that house, they would be alive now. Alive.*

The entire force of 2,000 Regulars faced Breed's Hill and the rebel fort. They waited quietly for General Howe to speak to them before sending them into battle. The general walked up and down the lines, slowly reviewing the troops. When he was done, he walked to the front and turned to address them all in a loud voice.

"Gentlemen! ... I am very happy to have the honor of commanding so fine a body of men. I know that you will behave like Englishmen and good soldiers. If the enemy will not come down from their fort, we must drive them out.

I shall not ask any of you to go a step further than where I go myself."

His speech finished, General Howe took his sword from its leather scabbard at his hip. As he turned his body toward Breed's Hill, he lifted the sword and pointed it at the rebel fort on the hill. Behind him, his army shouted one thunderous "HUZZAH!"

Will Pitcairn joined in the shouting. For the moment at least, it took his mind off the two deserters swinging from that tree.

CHAPTER TWELVE

Breed's Hill

"Here they come!" All along the American lines, officers barked out orders. The resting Patriots suddenly came to life. Waking from his nap, Barnabus Dunham stood up to join Danny Reed on the front wall's firing step.

Like the others around them, Barnabus and Danny looked out at those waves of red coats slowly coming up the hill. The Regulars marched in wide "ranks," or lines, each rank of marching soldiers a few steps behind the rank in its front. The top of each rank shimmered, as the sunlight reflected off their polished bayonets.

Danny's father had no time to waste watching the enemy's approach. He was busy doing his duties as lieutenant. First, he made sure each musketman had a spare flint, and enough musket balls and gunpowder. Next, he lined them up with the proper amount of space between them to prevent crowding.

Danny felt proud as he listened to his father review the

"manual of arms" with a nervous soldier. They had practiced these steps for loading and firing a musket countless times on the monthly muster day back home in Barre. That had been practice. In a few minutes the real test would come.

Though Danny was proud of his father, he was frustrated with his own role. A fifer is important when the company is on the march. But, right now, no one was calling for music. Danny wished he was a musketman, like some of his friends in the company.

They were only two or three years older. Danny knew he could shoot just as well as any of them. Many times he'd hunted with his father in the forests near their Barre home in western Massachusetts. By now, he had become quite good at bringing down deer and other game.

I will wait for the right time, he thought. *I'll watch for a free musket. Perhaps someone will get scared and desert. He'll leave his musket behind in his hurry to get away. I'll put it to good use. Father may not approve, but I dare not ask him. He might say no. I'll just take the musket up and use it. Worry about Father later. Once the firing starts, with all the smoke and confusion, he may not even notice.*

The British advanced slowly. About every fifty yards, they stopped to wait for the artillery to come up and fire off a few rounds of six pound balls. The army's advance was also slowed by fences and a marshy area. After each obstacle was overcome, the British officers took their time forming the ranks again. The officers insisted on perfect formations before advancing again.

Inside the fort, a man down the line from Danny couldn't take the tension anymore. He'd been watching the British start and stop, start and stop. When would they charge with those awful bayonets? He burst out, "Why don't they hurry up and get on with it!" Danny saw that the man's hands were shaking and he was sweating heavily.

Colonel Prescott was close by. He spoke to the man quietly. "Easy, man. Sit down and rest for a minute. ... That's it, rest now. Let them have their showy parade. We can wait.

"And when they approach," he continued, raising his voice so others could hear, "let us all remember to keep cool and hold our fire. Wait for my order."

Danny turned back to watching the Redcoats' approach. They had such perfect formations! Danny wondered what it would be like to wear one of those fancy British uniforms.

He couldn't hear any fifers, so he watched the British drummers. Some of them looked even younger than himself. Other drummers were grown men. They all seemed to be in harmony, giving the soldiers a slow beat to march to. Every Regular kept in step with the beat of the drums. It was an awesome spectacle.

A man standing a few places to Danny's left said, to no one in particular, "Those Britishers sure make a nice parade. Look so pretty in those fancy uniforms; I hate to bloody them all up by shooting at them."

Danny wasn't the only one who heard the man. Doctor Joseph Warren had, and he guessed what was troubling the man. He walked over, put a hand on the man's shoulder, and spoke to him.

"Friend, we all have a very hard duty to perform today. When you fire your gun, don't think about that man out there you're aiming at. Think about your loved ones back home not having to live any longer under the thumb of the British. Think about your children, and the children after them, living in freedom because you did your duty here today.

"It's not easy having to kill another man. I don't want to take lives either. But there comes a time when a people must rise up and say, 'Enough! We won't take any more!' That time is now, my friend."

The man nodded his head, then turned back to face the British with a more determined look on his face. Doctor Warren patted him on the shoulder and returned to his place in line.

General Pigot led the British left division towards the fort and its Massachusetts defenders. To Pigot's right, General Howe led the other British division towards the rail fence. There, on the slope that led down to the Mystic River, the defenders were from Connecticut and New Hampshire. The rail fence protected the fort from a "flank," or side, attack on the Mystic River side of Breed's Hill.

Soon after starting the advance, General Howe's division came to a swayle with a slight rise in front. While in this hollow, Howe's troops were hidden from the view of the Americans behind the rail fence in front of them. So he ordered them to halt here.

He ordered his fastest soldiers – the light infantry – to move off to the right and drop down the eight foot high bluff to the Mystic River beach below. There they reformed into a long column, because the beach was narrow. They were ordered to march along the beach until they passed the rebels up above at the rail fence. Then climb up the bluff, and attack them from behind.

Because General Howe was in a hollow, the Patriots at

the rail fence could not see what he'd just done. But Colonel Prescott, in the fort up on Breed's Hill, had seen it. He knew he must warn Colonel John Stark, the New Hampshire man in charge down at the rail fence. Tell him to watch out, because the British general was sending a flanking column of light infantry Regulars along the beach to surprise him.

Colonel Prescott did not want to weaken his own defense by ordering a musketman from the fort to carry the message to Stark. He called over all the officers who were inside the fort, and talked to them in private.

"... The messenger," he finished, "must be fast on his feet. And he must be someone who can be trusted to deliver the message, not run away."

At first, there was silence. Then the lieutenant from Barre spoke up. "Sir, I have someone in my company who can do it. He's a good shot, but not doing us much good today without a musket. And he's as swift as a deer."

Colonel Prescott looked Lieutenant Reed in the eye and challenged him, "Are you sure he can be trusted to deliver the message and not run away?"

Without blinking, Lieutenant Reed answered in a strong voice, "Yes, sir. He's my son."

CHAPTER THIRTEEN

Between Breed's Hill and Bunker Hill

B efore Danny Reed set out on his mission, he lightened himself as much as possible. In his father's care he left his fife, and his hat, coat and empty canteen. Danny's father gravely shook his hand.

"Godspeed, son. Be careful. Don't take any unnecessary chances."

Danny wanted to reply, but couldn't get the words out. He felt awkward standing there. All he could manage was a nod and a half smile before turning and running out the opening at the rear of the fort.

As he ran down the north side of Breed's Hill toward the rail fence, Danny was mad at himself. *I should have told Father that he, too, must be careful.*

While they'd been together in the fort, Danny hadn't thought very much about the danger they were in. The chance that his father might be killed before Danny returned filled his head now like a nightmare.

Frightened by the idea, Danny slowed his pace to a jog. As he went on, he looked down at the ground. He was trying to find something, anything, to focus on and free his mind of such thoughts.

Unlike the other side of the hill, these hayfields were mown. So it was easy for him to see the discarded belongings of the deserters. In their hurry to flee from danger, they had thrown away their knapsacks, coats, anything that might have slowed them down. Danny weaved in and out to avoid stepping on any of this litter.

He spotted a wooden canteen up ahead. It tempted him, and for a moment he stopped. But he thought better of it and kept on jogging, remembering how important his mission was. *Perhaps,* he thought, *after I deliver the message to Colonel Stark, I'll return this way and see if the canteen has anything left in it.*

His mind distracted by the canteen, Danny had taken his eyes off the ground. He did not see the skunk hole in front of him. His left foot fell in up to the shin. Stuck in the hole, his left ankle twisted. "Oww!" His other foot stumbled and he fell, landing hard on his left shoulder.

Danny lay on his back for a while, catching his breath. He felt like he could not possibly get up. He was light-headed from the hard work, the sun, nothing to eat or drink. Sleep called to him, tempting him to close his eyes. "No, no!" Danny said to himself. "I have to get up and keep moving. Deliver that message to Colonel Stark."

It was uncomfortable down here anyway. The ground was hot, and the stubble of freshly cut hay was prickly on the back of his sweaty neck. Danny sat up and put his head between his knees until the dizziness went away.

Then he tried standing up. "Oww!" A sharp, piercing shot of pain in his left ankle made him lose his balance and fall down again.

"Darn! I must have sprained it. ... Great!" Danny was disgusted, blaming himself for not watching where he was going.

He stood up again, this time being careful to put his weight on the other foot. Gingerly, he took a few steps, wincing each time he put any pressure on his bad foot. "I need a crutch of some kind."

Quickly looking around, Danny spotted the wooden canteen that had caught his eye earlier. He hopped towards it on his right foot, lost his balance, and fell down next to the canteen.

Shaking the wooden canteen, he heard faint splashing sounds inside. Not quite empty. He pulled out the stopper, and lifted the canteen up. When the water fell on his tongue, he tried gargling. This soothed his parched throat for a little while, before he let the water slide the rest of the way down.

Having tasted water once again, Danny thirsted for more. Closing his eyes, he pictured himself drinking quarts down without stopping. Then jumping in the ten foot hole in the river back home. And staying under till his whole body was cooled.

Only slightly refreshed by the water, Danny sighed, opened his eyes, and stood up. He let the canteen drop to the ground, and continued his search.

To his surprise, Danny soon found the perfect crutch – a musket! He used it to hobble around on his good foot, looking for either a cartridge box or a powder horn and bullet pouch.

But the deserter had only thrown away his musket. "Great!" Danny said out loud, "You're a messenger with a sprained ankle, and a musketman with no ammunition."

As he stood there feeling sorry for himself, a familiar hissing sound came from behind him. He turned around and, just for a split second, saw a cannon ball flying directly at him. Its hiss turned into a howl as the ball quickly came closer. Danny threw himself flat on the ground. An instant later, he felt the ground shake as the cannon ball landed with a thud a few feet behind him, and bounded away down the hill.

Danny lay on the ground panting. The fear had a hold on him now. Suddenly, he burst into a violent fit of sobbing. He cried out loud - great sobs that made his body shake. Tears made streaks down his dirty face.

Danny felt very alone and wished he was back in the fort with his father. Ashamed for crying like this, he rolled onto his stomach and hid his face in the grass. He knew now that he had been scared all along, even in the fort. It had been easy before to hide the fear. Father and Barnabus were there with him, and so was Colonel Prescott, and Doctor Warren - men who showed no fear. They'd all seemed safe enough behind the fort's walls.

Still shaking, Danny grabbed the musket and used it to push himself up, then leaned on it for balance. After wiping the tears from his eyes and cheeks, he nervously looked back over his shoulder. No more cannon balls.

Gripping the barrel of the musket with both hands, Danny set out again. He hobbled along as fast as he could towards the rail fence. Every few yards, he turned his head to glance back.

Finally, tired from hopping on one leg, Danny reached the rail fence. His ankle was throbbing now. Without his hat for shade, the sun seemed hotter than he could bear. He was dizzy and seeing stars now. Danny leaned the musket against the fence, and grabbed the top rail with both hands to steady himself.

"You all right there, sonny?" a voice asked him.

CHAPTER FOURTEEN

The Rail Fence

"I said, 'Are you all right, sonny?' You look mighty peekid."

Danny didn't know who was talking to him. He guessed it must be one of the men he'd seen as he approached the fence moments before. Danny kept his head down and his eyes closed, concentrating on not passing out. He answered the man without looking up.

"I'll be all right, I reckon, once I rest a bit. I have to talk to Colonel Stark."

"Ain't here," the man said. "I'll fetch over Captain Knowlton, instead. You can talk to him."

After a while, Danny felt less dizzy and opened his eyes. Staring at the ground, he focused on the stubble of freshly cut hay. Suddenly, someone grabbed his shoulder and Danny jumped.

"Son – look at me, son." Wide awake now, Danny lifted his head and stared at the man. "Son, I'm Captain Knowlton, from Connecticut. Someone said you have a message for Colonel Stark. Is it from Colonel Prescott?"

"Ye- yes, captain. I just came from the fort on Breed's Hill and –"

"Come," Knowlton interrupted. "Step off a minute with me and I'll hear it in private." Danny grabbed the musket and hobbled away with the captain.

Danny recited from memory Colonel Prescott's message about the British flanking party forming on the Mystic River beach. Captain Knowlton nodded his head and thanked Danny for delivering the message. "I'll have someone from my company carry your message to Colonel Stark. You can go back –"

"Please, sir," Danny objected. "I can make it. Honest I can. I have to get the message to Colonel Stark myself. I promised Colonel Prescott and my father I would."

Captain Knowlton frowned and nodded his head. "All right, son, though I believe Colonel Stark may not need that message. He's down there now preparing for them as we speak. If you're determined to go, I'll have someone carry your musket and lend you a shoulder to lean on."

He turned away for a moment and waved his arm. "Abiel! Over here!" Turning back to Danny, the captain smiled. "Here, son, wet your gullet a bit while you wait."

Danny was careful not to take more than a sip, then handed the canteen back. "Much obliged, sir."

A heavy-set, serious looking man in a white wig and long, black coat arrived and stood next to the captain. He gave the captain a questioning look, wanting to hear why he'd been called over.

Captain Knowlton introduced the man to Danny. "This is Reverend Abiel Leonard, from Woodstock, Connecticut."

Captain Kowlton introduced the man to Danny.

Captain Knowlton continued, "He is the chaplain for our regiment, son."

Reverend Leonard turned to stare at Danny with deep, penetrating eyes, as if he was searching Danny's soul for sins.

"Rev- reverend," Danny said nervously, nodding his head.

Danny wished the chaplain would say something, turn back to the captain, do anything – just stop looking at him like that. He knew that kind of look, remembered it from going to Meeting on Sundays back in Barre. The thought came to Danny that perhaps to be a reverend you have to be able to look right through a person.

A familiar, uncomfortable feeling of guilt came over Danny. It was like the way he'd often felt back home in church on Sundays. He'd be sitting in one of those straight-backed hard pews. Danny would squirm, but he never could escape those knowing eyes of the reverend.

Nearly every Sunday, those harsh eyes seemed to find Danny's, and stay there staring at him. A few inches lower than those harsh eyes, an equally harsh mouth barked out warnings. Warnings – for all wicked sinners – of eternal damnation in the fires of hell. Danny always felt certain those warnings were meant for him alone. Now this strange man from Connecticut was giving him that same stare.

"Abiel," Captain Knowlton said finally. "This is ..."

"Uh, Danforth Reed, sir. Barre, Massachusetts Company."

"Abiel, I'd like you to assist this young man to the other end of the line. Seems he twisted his ankle. But he's set his mind on delivering a message to Colonel Stark."

The chaplain stopped staring now and smiled at Danny. "Glad to make your acquaintance, son," he said cheerily.

"Give me that gun to carry." He came around to Danny's left side, took the musket, and held Danny up for a moment. "Now, just drape that left arm of yours over my shoulders. ... There. Ready? Let's go."

They had about 200 yards of rail fence to walk before they would reach the end of the line and find Colonel Stark. They passed the time talking as they walked. Like most preachers, the chaplain liked to hear himself talk.

First, they discussed each side's chances in the battle that was about to begin. Danny did most of the listening. He was surprised that a preacher could be so interested in war. Finally, Danny got up the nerve to ask something that was puzzling him.

"Reverend Leonard, may I ask you something?"

"Of course, my son."

"Well, why is it that you – a man of peace – are with us here today? Are you planning on fighting, sir?"

The chaplain nodded his head and smiled. "A very good question, Danforth. Yes, I do indeed plan to do my share of the fighting. Not only on this day, but in all the other battles to follow. If it be the will of the Lord that I live so long.

"This America we're building is like a city of light on a hill. Put here as an example for all the Lord's peoples to look upon. We must, therefore, be a good people and stop our sinful ways. And we must defeat in battle all evil men that sin against us.

"That is why we are here today – to call forth our wicked enemies, call them to the field of battle. And make them feel the mighty sword of the Lord! For we know that we go into battle with the Lord at our side. We come from the original chosen people of the Lord, the Israelites of old. You know that, don't you, son?"

"Oh yes, reverend. I read my Bible, sir."

"As for myself," Reverend Leonard continued, "I have left my home and joined our Patriot army because it is my duty I owe to my country. It matters not if I live or die – my life is in God's hands. I take up a musket today to do the Lord's work, for the glory of God and the good of America.

"So, take heart young man – you are doing the Lord's work. As Joab, the leader of King David's armies, said to his chosen soldiers before going into battle: 'Be strong and courageous! Let us fight hard for our people and for the cities of our God. And may the Lord's will be done!' Amen."

"Amen," echoed Danny.

Danny and Reverend Leonard walked the rest of the way in silence, Danny thinking about the chaplain's words. They stopped when they reached the bluff. There the ground dropped down sharply to the beach eight feet below.

CHAPTER FIFTEEN

Mystic River Beach

L ooking down at the beach directly below them, Danny and the reverend saw that Colonel Stark was ready and waiting for the British flanking column. The long column of marching Redcoats was now less than 100 yards away.

Behind a quickly made low stone wall, Stark had lined up his best marksmen in three tightly packed ranks of 50 each. A few had muskets, but most had the longer barreled "rifle-guns." None of them had bayonets.

Each rifleman had one knee on the ground. Some of the men were checking their weapons one last time. The rest were watching the Redcoats coming down the narrow beach.

With a touch of disappointment in his voice, Danny said to Reverend Leonard, "I guess I don't need to tell Colonel Stark that message after all."

"That's right, son. But you did right well to hobble all the way down here anyhow. Just lay yourself down and watch the action below us. Keep your head down." They both laid on their stomachs on the grass near the edge of the bluff.

The British column came to a halt. For a few moments there was a tense silence. All eyes were on the British officer at the front of the column. "Fix, bayonet!" he rang out loud and clear, cutting the stillness. This was followed by the metallic sounds of 300 bayonets, as each British light infantryman locked his bayonet onto the end of his musket.

Danny heard Colonel Stark speak to his men in a calm and quiet voice. "Steady now, boys. Check your guns. And remember, remain still and hold your fire till I give the word. Then we'll show them what New Hampshire can do."

Kneeling behind their low stone wall, they faced their enemy. Mouths were dry now, and heartbeats were racing. Their minds were thinking about those awful bayonets, 17 inches of cold steel coming their way. Sweat flowed down their bodies like rain. It blurred their eyesight and wet their hands – those same hands and eyes that must work right and not fail them now.

"Present arms! ... Fire!" The first three British ranks stuck out their muskets without aiming, and fired a volley at Stark's sharpshooters. Only one American was hit.

"Charge, bayonet!" With their bayoneted muskets lowered to waist height, 300 British voices rose in one loud "HUZZAH!" The column moved forward at a run.

Danny was frightened. "They're getting close, reverend! Why don't we fire?"

The chaplain pointed. "Just keep your eye on that wooden stake, son, sticking out of the sand down there. Colonel Stark put it there for a reason."

They were closing in on a wooden stake that Stark had planted in the sand earlier. It was forty "paces," or marching steps, from Stark's first rank – so close his marksmen couldn't miss. Stark had told them not to fire until the first Regular reached the wooden stake.

Now it was Colonel Stark's turn to bark out orders.

"Front rank, make ready!" All together, the first rank of defenders stood up just behind the low stone wall.

"Take aim!" Muskets and rifles were carefully aimed at the charging Redcoats. They were up to the wooden stake now.

"Fire!" The first rank of American marksmen squeezed their triggers. Bullets flew through the air like rain falling sideways. Lead balls tore through uniforms and skin, smashing into organs and bones. Sounds of bones breaking and screams filled the air.

The injured Redcoats were thrown back by the force of the bullets. They fell backwards, stumbling into their comrades behind them and they all fell down together. Slippery, sticky blood spurted from their wounds, staining the uniforms of those who weren't even injured yet.

Over the screams of the wounded, British officers yelled at those soldiers who were not injured. "Form ranks! FORM RANKS!" They must line up, so they can resume their charge.

One Redcoat, instead of forming in line, lifted his musket and fired at the rebels. An officer quickly reached out and struck him with the flat of his sword. "Stop firing! Wait till you're close enough to use your bayonet, lad. Form ranks, lads!"

Behind their stone wall, the front rank of New Hampshire marksmen had returned to their kneeling position to begin reloading. One man just stood there after firing and watched the Redcoats trying to reform. His neighbor reached up and pulled his arm. "Fool, get down and reload! This ain't no parade you're watching."

Other men, nervous and hurrying, fumbled and swore as they tried to reload. They had practiced it so many times back home on muster day! Why couldn't their fingers and minds work right?

John Stark quietly counted off the seconds while keeping his eye on the British. Time enough. "Second rank, make ready!" His second rank of sharpshooters stood up together. They prepared to fire over the heads of the kneelers in front.

"Take aim!" yelled Stark. They focused in on the new targets, the newly formed up ranks of Redcoats.

"Charge!" yelled a new British officer who had taken over command.

"Fire!" yelled John Stark a second later.

Again the charging British were struck down. They still were not more than a few feet past the wooden stake that Stark had stuck in the sand. After this second volley, the wooden stake could no longer be seen. The stake was now in splinters, and buried beneath a growing pile of bodies.

"Form ranks! Form ranks!" Some of the Redcoats still standing turned to run away. They were willing to risk any punishment, rather than face such deadly fire again. Officers shouted threats of instant death for deserters. They hit them with the flat sides of their swords and forced them back into line.

"Charge!" The Redcoats came on for the third time, stepping over the dead bodies at their feet.

By now, Stark's third rank was ready and taking aim. "Fire!"

A shower of lead struck the Redcoats once again, toppling them onto the fallen bodies already on the ground. All those who survived this third fire turned and ran or limped back down the beach. Their officers in the rear could not stop them. The Redcoats didn't stop until they reached Moulton's Point, where they had landed when they'd come over from Boston.

A cheer went up from the Americans on the beach and those watching above. Reverend Leonard stood up and spoke out in a loud voice, "The Egyptians said, 'Let us flee from the face of Israel, for the Lord fighteth for them against us.'"

Danny Reed said nothing. He remained lying on the grass, stunned, staring down at the dead bodies on the beach directly below him. He saw dozens of twisted bodies. Some were silent; others were moaning and crying for help. They lay one on top of another in heaps separated by patches of blood-stained sand.

Danny could not take his eyes off them. Tears streamed down his cheeks.

CHAPTER SIXTEEN

Boston

Across the Charles River, the battle was being watched by thousands of people in Boston. They looked out their upstairs windows, climbed onto their roofs, any place to get a good view of the battle.

Eben Dunham and his mother Lydia were still in the cupola atop their house. They could not see the action on the Mystic River beach. But, closer to Boston, they could see Pigot's Regulars marching up Breed's Hill towards the Patriot fort high above the village of Charlestown.

"Isn't it grand, Mother?" Eben asked.

Lydia did not answer. She was thinking about her husband Barnabus. *Is he over there, one of the Patriots defending that fort? Perhaps I will watch Barnabus die this afternoon and not even know it.*

"Oh, look, Mother! Near Charlestown, do you see it? Redcoats are falling down. I hear the muskets, but I don't see any smoke coming from our fort. How can that be? Who is shooting at them?"

Lydia wished her son would be quiet and stop asking her so many questions. She did not want to watch this awful scene. But she could not force herself to leave the cupola and go downstairs.

"Oh, I don't know, Eben" she answered him. "Perhaps we have men somewhere outside the fort."

Eben thought about it. "Yes, perhaps so. I remember now! I saw some of our troops leave the fort a couple hours ago. I think they disappeared into Charlestown's upper streets. Do you remember, Mother? ... Yes, look there."

Eben pointed at Charlestown. "Doesn't that look like gunsmoke drifting up from some of those houses? That's it! We must have snipers there, shooting at the British."

Nervous, Lydia walked around the inside of the tiny room again. She stopped by the window where they'd seen the British cannons near their house. "Eben – Eben, another messenger is riding up the hill."

"Oh, help me over, please," he asked. "I want to listen again."

She moved his chair to the window and helped Eben hobble over to it. His bandaged feet still hurt with each step, but he hardly noticed the pain. His mind was too focused on all that was going on.

The British messenger halted his horse in front of the two generals and the artillery officer. He talked to them from horseback for just a few moments.

Eben opened the window, stuck his head out, and strained his ears once again to listen. He faintly picked up a few words: "... snipers ... Charlestown ... Howe orders ... burn ..." Turning his horse around, the messenger rode back down the hill.

The artillery officer shouted orders to his men, something about "carcasses." Eben didn't know what carcasses were, but he guessed this was not good news. He decided not to tell his mother what he'd heard. She was upset enough already. Eben hoped he was wrong about what he guessed was about to happen.

He did not have to wait long to find out. He watched the artillerymen first lower the barrels of their guns. Next, they brought over metal cans instead of balls. These hollow cans, with holes punched in them to let in air, were filled with burning rags. They were meant to set fire to their targets.

Eben clearly heard the artillery officer this time, as he shouted, "Fire at will!"

BOOM! ... BOOM! ... BOOM!

Eben watched the carcasses fly through the air high over the Charles River and disappear in Charlestown. Many of them landed on the roofs of the houses. Less than a minute later, he saw first smoke, then flames, rising from the houses.

Shouts went up from the spectators all over Boston. Hearing them, Lydia Dunham looked out and saw the flames and smoke across the river. She shrieked, "Oh, my God! They are burning the town! Lord, help us against these evil men."

Soon the fire spread to the churches. The tall steeples sent flames reaching for the sky.

CHAPTER SEVENTEEN

The Rail Fence

olonel John Stark, carefully inspecting the dead and wounded, called for a chaplain. Reverend Abiel Leonard climbed down the bluff to the beach. The colonel asked him to comfort a British soldier who was dying of his wounds. The soldier turned out to be a boy not much older than Danny.

Danny watched as Reverend Leonard held the British boy's head and shoulders in his lap and prayed aloud for him. "Lord, into your hands I deliver the soul of this fine young man. Accept him, Lord. Amen."

The boy breathed his last breath, and his whole body shuddered as he died in the chaplain's arms. Reverend Leonard gently laid the boy's head on the chest of another dead soldier, then lovingly brushed the hair out of the boy's face. Before leaving, he closed the boy's eyelids and placed a coin over each one. This would keep off the sun until the boy's comrades could return for him.

After climbing back up the bluff, the chaplain saw that Danny was standing now. "Danforth, if you're going to return to the fort sometime today, we'd best be heading out. Here," he said, as he took Danny's musket from him and offered a shoulder to lean on, "I'll help you as far as the end of this fence."

"Thank you, reverend," Danny said absently without looking up. His face was pale as he kept staring at the dead boy on the beach. "Was – was that soldier –" Danny couldn't finish. Tears again ran down his cheeks.

"Best not think on it, son. He's on his way to Paradise now. Let's go."

They walked nearly the whole length of the fence before they were stopped by a man kneeling on the ground. The man, looking up at them, wildly waved his hand up and down. "Reverend Leonard! Get your head down! You're an easy target standing up like that. Can't you see those lobsterbacks are coming up to firing range?"

The chaplain looked out at the British, sighed, and handed Danny the musket.

"I best be seeing to my own gun, Danforth. I'll be taking my leave of you now, so I can return to my post. You'd be wise to set yourself down here for a spell. It appears the British don't want you to make it all the way back to the fort quite yet."

He shook Danny's hand in a manly way. "Go with God, Danforth." Turning around, he ran back down the line.

Danny barely managed to get out a weak "Thank you" as the chaplain ran off. Danny watched Reverend Leonard stop, kneel down, and pick up a musket.

"You're welcome to join me down here."

"Huh?" Danny said, as he turned to look down at the speaker. It was the man kneeling on the ground who had spoken to the chaplain before, warning him to get down.

"I said, 'You're welcome to join me.' But you better make up your mind right quick, before you get yourself killed. Only someone with addled brains – or maybe a Redcoat that don't know no better – would stand up with no cover during a battle. Lead's gonna be flying mighty thick any second now. Better set yourself down, like the good reverend said."

Danny glanced out at the British in front of them, then stared up at the fort for a moment, thinking of his father. Frowning, he nodded his head to the man on the ground. By leaning his weight on his musket, Danny eased himself down. He settled on his behind and his right leg to keep his weight off his bad left ankle.

Danny smiled and offered the man his hand. "Thank you, sir. I'm Danforth Reed, Barre, Massachusetts Company."

The man smiled and shook his hand firmly. "Don't call me 'sir'. Name's Bradford – Bradford Newcomb. I hail from Lebanon, down Connecticut way. Welcome to my fence." He laughed at his own joke, and turned his attention back to the approaching Redcoats.

There was a little hole in the fence that he could look and shoot through. It was a double fence – two zig-zag, "worm" rail fences that the Patriots had set a foot apart, then stuffed hay between. Danny made a hole, too, and peered out at the enemy.

They were less than a hundred yards away now, Danny guessed. He could not believe how huge they were. They made him wish he was back in the fort with his father and Barnabus. Danny wasn't too sure this fence offered much protection. *How am I going to defend myself without a bayonet?* he thought. *I won't be able to outrun them with this sprained ankle.*

The Redcoats came on, led by the tallest soldiers in the British army. These special troops, called "grenadiers," wore very high helmets on their heads, which made them look even taller. Just looking at them coming towards him made Danny wish he was someplace else.

Even from this distance, Danny could see that the British soldiers were sweating badly, even their officers. The flour that British officers used to powder their hair was mixing with sweat from their scalps. It made funny looking white streaks run down their faces. The officers didn't wipe their faces, though. It would not be proper to let soldiers see their officer wiping his face while marching against the enemy.

Danny jumped, startled by the sound of a single musket. It was fired by a Patriot a few places up the line who was too nervous to wait for the order to fire. Within moments, Danny heard hoof beats approaching. He looked up and saw General Israel Putnam reining in his snorting white horse.

Waving his sword above his head, the red-faced general declared, "The next man who fires without orders shall lose his head to the edge of this sword!" That said, "Old Put" quickly calmed down and talked to the troops.

"We don't have powder and ball to waste at this distance, boys. So, wait for your officer's orders. Be cool, and hold your fire till you see the whites of their eyes. Take your time, and *squeeze* the trigger slowly, don't pull it. Look for the handsome uniforms, the ones with the gold epaulets on their shoulders – pick off the officers first."

He went off down the line to repeat the advice to others.

CHAPTER EIGHTEEN

Breed's Hill

Inside the fort, Colonel Prescott used a calm voice to speak to his tired, nervous Patriots. "Keep your bodies and muskets below the wall, out of sight of the British, till I give the word."

In front of them, General Pigot's line continued its march up the hill. The Regulars wore stiff, high collars that forced their chins to stay up, making their faces look into the sun behind the rebel fort.

These Redcoats were full of spirit as they marched up the hill. They didn't expect the Yankee rebels to put up much of a fight. A soldier marching near Will Pitcairn cried out, "Push on! Let us get at the dogs!" Another one yelled, "Remember Concord! Time to get even, lads."

Will Pitcairn was sure that, once the Redcoats got over the walls and put their bayonets to work, the Yankees would run away. They were all cowards, everyone knew that.

They were only fifty yards from the ditch now. Will could

not see any Yankee heads above the walls. *The Yankees have all run away,* he thought. *Cowards!*

Suddenly, Will heard a voice from inside the fort. "Make ready!" Hundreds of musket barrels rose up and settled atop the walls, pointing at Will and the other Redcoats. It surprised Will. A sudden fear gripped him. He stopped marching for a second. "Father –"

"Keep *moving,* son. We must keep moving. Stay close to me. I'll protect you."

Will nodded his head and kept marching, though his legs were suddenly wobbly. His face was pale now, and his breathing came in puffs. Sweat poured down his forehead into his eyes. He tried to blink it away so he could see. This was not at all what he'd expected. Those rebel guns were pointed right at him.

"Charge, bayonet!" General Pigot yelled.

"HUZZAH!" answered back more than a thousand Regulars. With their bayoneted muskets leveled in front of them, they started their run. This was the awesome and deadly British bayonet charge that had beaten the best French armies in the last war. Surely, it could beat American rebels. Surely.

Will heard the same American voice again. "Take aim! ... Fire!"

The long line of muskets belched bright yellow flames, then white smoke. To Ebenezer Dunham, watching from Boston, the firing sounded like the roll of a hundred drums. He saw the long line of Redcoats fall to the ground like dominos in a row.

Only a few men from Pigot's front rank remained standing. The rest were down on the ground. Many of them lay still, lifeless. The others made a frightful scene of wounded bodies screaming and thrashing on the ground.

The second rank suddenly found they had become the front rank. Those officers who were still standing worked hard and quickly to bring order to the line. They reformed it to resume the charge. "Form ranks! Form ranks, lads!" John and Will Pitcairn moved up, stepping over their fallen comrades.

Will saw the rebel muskets disappear behind the wall – to reload, he guessed. Others quickly appeared in their place, ready to take their turn.

Volley after volley came at them from the walls, not allowing them to reform and charge. Instead, Will Pitcairn and the Regulars all around him stood in place and began firing back. This went on for ten to fifteen minutes. Finally, they turned and ran back down the hill.

As he retreated, Will could hear the rebels behind him shouting, "Huzzah!" One of them raised his voice to yell above the others, "Are the Yankees cowards now?"

CHAPTER NINETEEN

The Rail Fence

D own at the rail fence, Danny watched the British march. They were almost to a fence about 50 yards in front of him.

"Make ready!" Danny knew that voice – it was Captain Knowlton's. Bradford, next to Danny, raised a musket.

The Redcoats were at the fence now. "Take aim! ... Fire!"

General Howe's Regulars had no chance facing hundreds of rebel musketmen taking turns. They tried to ignore the American fire and climb over the fence. But it was too hard to do with their heavy packs on their backs. So they gave up trying, and stood behind the fence firing their muskets at the Yankees 50 yards away.

Most of their balls, though, went over the Yankees' heads. The British had been taught to not take the time to aim. No, just stick your guns out in front of your bodies, everyone pull the trigger at the same time, then charge with your bayonet right away. Their orders had been to receive the enemy's first fire, then charge with the bayonet.

But the Redcoats were not charging now – just standing in place, firing, reloading, and firing again. They all ignored their officers who tried to make them stop firing and charge.

"Captain Baldwin's hit!" Danny and Bradford turned to see. The New Hampshire captain had been firing his own musket while standing up to lead his men, when he was hit by British fire. Baldwin managed to fire off his own gun three more times before collapsing to the ground. A couple of his men picked him up. As they set out to take their dying captain to the rear, he gave his company parting words.

"You'll beat them, boys. I'll be back, just as soon as the doctor treats this."

Danny hadn't fired a gun yet. He watched Bradford reload and noticed that the man was using "buck and ball" – a musket ball and a few pieces of buckshot. As he watched Bradford, a British musket ball came through the fence and hit Bradford in the arm. "Unh!"

Fortunately, it was just a flesh wound, going right through the arm without hitting bone. Danny knew what to do. He tore Bradford's sleeve off, then used it as a tourniquet to stop the bleeding.

"Much obliged, son. I won't be much of a marksman now with the use of only one arm. Here, take my gun. Yes, go on. Can you shoot?"

"Y- yes. I'm a right good shot sometimes, when I hunt deer with my father."

"Well, we're hunting lobsterbacks today," he said gravely, looking Danny in the eye. "Better be a sure shot. We can't afford to miss."

Danny nodded and took the musket from Bradford, who

"Here, take my gun."

offered some advice. "It tends to the left a might. Take that into account when you aim."

Danny noticed his stomach was more than a bit queasy as he lifted the barrel over the rail and through the hole he had made in the hay. He was glad he could rest the heavy gun on a rail, because his hands were shaking badly. From habit, he rested the butt end of the musket firmly against his shoulder. That way it wouldn't bruise him when he fired.

Danny had trouble seeing through all the smoke. From what he could tell, though, it looked like the British were rallying. An officer wearing a fancy coat trimmed with gold waved a sword in one hand and shouted to the Redcoats all around him.

Danny took aim at the man's middle. He tried to steady his wet, shaking hands as his finger very, very slowly squeezed the gun's trigger. As he did, he watched the man opening and closing his mouth. Danny could almost hear what the man was shouting.

Danny was surprised when his own gun went off. He'd forgotten he was squeezing the trigger. The explosion rocked him back a bit. But he kept his eye on the British officer he'd aimed at.

Danny saw the sword drop from the man's hand. His arms seemed to quickly fly up and backwards. A patch of red suddenly appeared on the man's chest, breaking through the whiteness of his vest. His mouth opened once more, and the look on his face changed to one of shocked surprise. He fell backwards, landing on his back.

The Redcoats stopped and stood still, unsure what to do. Too many of their officers had been taken out of the action. There weren't enough officers left to shout orders to them, make decisions for them, and lead them. First a few, then the rest, turned and ran back towards Moulton's Point.

All along the rail fence, shouts of triumph and joy went up. "Huzzah!" "Take that, you dirty Redcoats!" "Go on back to England!"

It seemed like all the men and boys behind the rail fence were celebrating. All except Danny Reed. To him, the screams of the wounded Redcoats seemed louder than the gunfire had earlier.

The man he had shot was dead, but Danny did not know it. It was a wounded Redcoat lying near the dead officer who was screaming. But Danny thought it was the man he'd shot. Danny turned away and covered his ears with his hands. Bobbing his head up and down, he cried out, "Make him stop! Make him stop! Can't someone make him stop?"

Bradford Newcomb stood up, climbed over the rails, and walked forward. He had no trouble finding the man who was screaming. The man lay on his back, dying. Bradford could see three separate bullet wounds in the man's chest. Bradford, using his good arm, slipped his tomahawk from his belt, then brought it swiftly down, hitting the top of the man's skull. The screams stopped.

CHAPTER TWENTY

At the bottom of Breed's Hill, Generals Howe and Pigot scolded their troops, telling them they should be ashamed for running away from Yankee rebels. Within five minutes, they were on the march again.

The second attack lasted about thirty minutes, twice as long as the first. But again the British Regulars stopped their charge and stood firing at the rebels. And, once again, they turned around and ran back down the hill.

In front of the rail fence, the retreating Redcoats left Major John Small standing there all alone – he had not noticed that his men had turned back. The American general, Israel Putnam, saw Major Small on the battlefield and remembered him. They had served together 20 years before in the French and Indian War.

Glancing to his left, Putnam saw three Patriots taking aim at Small. Putnam spurred his horse, quickly reached them, and struck their musket barrels down with his sword. "Do not kill that man! I love him like a brother." Major Small bowed to his old friend, and turned to catch up with his retreating Redcoats.

Many of the wounded Regulars were rowed back to Boston. Their boats landed right below Copp's Hill. Eben and Lydia Dunham looked straight down and saw them. The bottoms of the boats were bright red from spilled blood.

New British troops, looking very pale and scared, waited on Boston's shore. After helping unload the wounded, they climbed into those same bloody boats. Then they rowed themselves across the river for their own turn to march against the Yankees. Many British and Tory women – wives and girlfriends of the soldiers – were also on hand. They yelled to their men, "Kill the Yankee rebels, my brave lads! Give it to them!"

In the second attack, Danny Reed and Bradford Newcomb had worked as a team. Danny, still feeling terrible about the man he had killed, refused to shoot any more. Because Bradford had been shot in one arm, he asked Danny to at least help him. Danny held up the musket for him while with his good arm Bradford took aim and squeezed the trigger.

After that second British attack ended in another British retreat, Danny and Bradford left the rail fence together. He lent Danny a shoulder to lean on as the reverend had done before. Danny left his musket behind. Bradford brought his own musket along, slung over his back on a leather strap. In the hand of his good arm, he carried the sword of the officer Danny killed.

As the British prepared to advance for the third time, Danny and Bradford hobbled into the fort up on Breed's Hill. They went to see Colonel Prescott right away. They felt they should tell him what happened on the beach and at the rail fence.

Colonel Prescott thanked Danny absently. His mind was on other things at the moment. He needed to check the very low supply of gunpowder and bullets. To Danny, it seemed that the colonel had forgotten about his mission - to warn Colonel Stark about the British column on the beach. *He doesn't have any idea of all the trouble I had running his errand,* Danny thought with disgust.

Danny wasn't able to think about it for long, though. His father and cousin Barnabus spotted him and came running over. Danny was surprised that his father would hug him in public like this. But Danny hugged him back just as hard.

"I knew you would make it, son," said Lieutenant Reed. "But I can't say I didn't worry a bit while you were gone." Danny noticed a tear coming down from one of his father's eyes. The tear picked up soot as it ran down his father's powder-blackened face. Danny thought the tear looked like a drop of dirty water.

"I was worried about you, too, Father." They were both smiling broadly now.

"You look like you've been through a lot," said Cousin Barnabus Dunham. Danny just nodded his head.

His father had noticed Danny's limp and that this man was holding him up. "Son, you'll have to tell me how you hurt yourself. But first, introduce me to this gentleman. I'm sure we owe him much for helping you."

After introducing Bradford Newcomb, Danny told his father about spraining his ankle in the skunk hole. And also about being helped along by first the chaplain then Bradford.

"Well, son. I think you've had enough fighting for one day. It's time you made your way back to camp for some well earned rest."

Turning to Bradford, Danny's father continued. "And you, sir, I thank for helping my son. It looks like you'll be wanting a doctor to tend that wound. Doctor Warren's here, but we've had our share of wounds, so he's powerful busy. There's sure to be plenty of doctors on the safe side of Charlestown Neck. Can I ask you to help my son one more time by bringing him back to camp?"

Danny didn't want to stay and kill any more Redcoats. But he couldn't bear to leave again and not know if his father was safe. He gathered his courage. He had never spoken back to his father before.

"Father, I'm staying here with you. Sir."

Joseph Reed had a strange and awful look on his face. Danny held his breath, waiting for his father to speak.

"Danforth, don't argue with me. I'm order–"

"Lieutenant!" Bradford jumped in, throwing his hands out. "Lieutenant Reed – may I make a request, sir? Both Danforth and myself are plumb wore out, him from limping and me from bleeding. Might we be permitted to stay here a short while, to rest ourselves a bit, you know, before we start out again?"

Danny's father did not appreciate this interference and was about to say so. But, just then, Colonel Prescott's hoarse voice was heard over all others. "Here they come again! Everyone to your posts! To your posts!"

Bradford helped Danny follow his father and Barnabus to the firing step. They would stay in the fort a little longer.

CHAPTER TWENTY-ONE

D anny looked down at the British army coming up the hill once again. He could hear some of them shouting as they came on. "Conquer or die!"

A nervous Patriot with a powder-blackened face came over to see Danny's father. "Lieutenant, most of us have only enough gunpowder left to fire off one, maybe two shots. And some of us, like me, don't have any musket balls left. Do you think we should ask Colonel Prescott to order a retreat? "

Lieutenant Reed ignored the question of retreat and told the man, "Look about your feet. There's plenty of small stones the size of a musket ball. They'll have to do. "

The man took his advice and dropped to the ground, searching on his hands and knees for pebbles. Others, seeing this, did likewise. They scrambled back to their posts, though, when they heard Colonel Prescott shout, "Make ready!"

"… Take aim!"

The British marched up the hill without stopping to fire their muskets this time. As they moved through the field, the blood-stained hay painted red streaks on their white knee britches. They were determined to climb over those walls and make the rebels pay. They were nearly at the ditch now.

"Fire!" yelled Colonel Prescott at the top of his lungs. A blast of fire at point blank range struck the charging soldiers with terrible effect. But they kept coming. They wouldn't be turned back this time.

On the Charlestown side of the fort, Major John Pitcairn was trying to lead his Marines around the fort. "Will, help me keep the men moving. We've got to get in the fort's rear. Close off the rebels' escape route."

As he spoke, Pitcairn's Marines were hit by a shower of flying lead that cut many of them down. They stopped running, and began firing their weapons at the heads above the wall.

"Stop firing!" Major Pitcairn screamed in anger. "Keep moving! They're leaving their fort!" A few of the Patriots, having fired their last shot, were indeed sneaking out the rear.

A boy at the wall, hearing Major Pitcairn, shouted back at him, "We are not all gone yet!" Standing next to the boy was a free black man named Salem Prince. Prince fired his musket at Major Pitcairn and hit him in the head. He slumped to the ground.

"Father!" Will dropped his musket, and threw himself on the ground next to his father. Will cried as he held his father's dead body in his arms. Looking at the Marines nearby, Will told them, "I've lost my father!"

They felt the same loss. John Pitcairn had been like a father to them for many years. One of them passed the word along, "We've lost our father."

With the help of three other Marines, Will lifted his father up and carried his body down through the Charlestown streets to the shore. Wading into the water, they placed the major in one of the boats of dead and wounded heading back to Boston. A tearful Will Pitcairn kissed his father for the last time, then returned to the battle.

While they were gone, the Marines' Adjutant Waller saw a captain also get hit by a Yankee and fall down. Waller feared that they would all be picked off if they stayed there much longer. They must cross that ditch!

He ran over to British Colonel Nesbitt and yelled in his ear, "Sir, if you will form your line on my left, we will try to go over the wall."

Nesbitt nodded his head yes. Covered by Nesbitt's line, Waller ran up and down the line of firing Marines and made them stop firing. After Waller formed them for a charge, he yelled, "Over the walls! Do it for Major Pitcairn!" The Marines leaped the ditch under the last of the rebels' fire and scrambled onto the wall.

Redcoats were coming over all the walls now. And they were finally putting their bayonets to use. Defenders without bayonets used shovels, sticks of wood, pitchforks, and the butt ends of their muskets to protect themselves against the British bayonets.

Danny Reed was still in the fort, alongside his father. Danny decided to defend himself. He had to. He took up a dead Patriot's gun. It wasn't loaded. He poured gunpowder down the barrel, and started using the ramrod to push a musket ball down the barrel. Then, looking up, Danny saw a Redcoat aiming a gun at him!

Danny had no time to think. He quickly lifted the musket and fired, though he hadn't finished loading yet – the ramrod was still in the barrel. The ramrod flew the few feet in the air and hit the Redcoat in the chest.

The Redcoat groaned, grabbed the ramrod, and pulled it out. Pulling the ramrod out took the last strength he had left and he died as he fell. He fell off the wall, face forward, landing on top of Danny. He was a big man, and his weight knocked Danny down. Danny fell to the ground with the dead Redcoat on top of him.

"RETREAT! RETREAT!" Colonel Prescott yelled. Too many British were pouring over the walls now, at last putting their bayonets to work.

"Let's go, Danny!" It was his father. Danny squirmed beneath the dead weight of the Redcoat. The smell of the man's fresh blood frightened Danny.

His father and Barnabus reached down and pulled the dead man off him, then jerked Danny upright. His feet barely touched the ground, as his father and Barnabus kept hold of his arms and hurried him along.

The dust and smoke made it so dark they had to feel the back wall with their hands, searching for the narrow opening. They finally found it and made their way out, bumping bodies in the crush of Patriots trying to escape. Luckily, they did not lose their balance, or else they would have been trampled for sure.

They heard Dr. Warren's voice. He was shouting orders to those who stayed behind with him, "Cover the retreat!" Together, they were holding off the British so most of the Patriots could escape. Another voice: "Warren – come on!

You can't stay here!" The good doctor shouted back, "I'll be along directly! Save yourselves!"

Outside the fort, Danny hopped along on his good leg as fast as he could. He was held up on either side by his father and cousin Barnabus. They each carried a musket in their free hand. Bradford had left his behind after cracking its wooden stock on the skull of a British Regular. Now he jogged alongside, carrying the British sword he'd picked up. He was ready to defend them with it, if need be.

The British were surprised that the rebels fought while retreating, inch by inch, in hand to hand combat. Here the Yankees were suffering their worst losses of the battle. Colonel Prescott stepped along with his sword up; blocking bayonet thrusts that missed his body but cut his coat in several places.

"Yankee rebel!" Bradford turned just in time to see the speaker. It was a British officer coming at him with a sword held high and about to strike. To defend himself, Bradford raised his own sword. It deflected the blow a bit. The British officer's sword missed its mark. It only cut through Bradford's shirt and grazed his other arm.

Because the sword did not hit its target, it threw the British officer off balance. Here was Bradford's chance. He quickly brought his own sword down on the man's arm, knocking him to the ground.

Bradford did not strike the man again. Instead, he kept moving. He looked back at the British officer on the ground and yelled, "That will teach you to match swords with a 'Yankee rebel!' Ha!"

A short ways further, Barnabus stopped suddenly, letting go of Danny's arm. "Joseph, I've got to go back."

"What!" Danny's father exclaimed.

"Yes. I have to get Doctor Warren out of there."

"Barnabus, don't be fool–"

"He's too important to the Cause! The whole movement will suffer without him. We can't risk him being captured. I'm going back. Don't come with me. Save yourselves." Barnabus ran off.

"Wait! Come back, Barnabus!" Joseph Reed watched him go for a few moments, then stamped his foot on the ground and swore, over and over. Danny had never heard his father swear before, but knew that if ever there could be a time for it, in the Lord's eyes, this must be it. Danny, too, worried for cousin Barnabus.

"Come on, son," his father said wearily. "We have to keep moving." Bradford Newcomb took Barnabus Dunham's place, and the three of them continued on towards Bunker Hill.

Danny, his father, and Bradford passed Bunker Hill, kept going, and crossed Charlestown Neck under a heavy fire from the British war ships.

They made it safely back to camp, all of them except Cousin Barnabus Dunham. The American camp was full of shouting Patriots. "To arms! To arms!" "The Regulars are coming!"

But the British didn't cross over Charlestown Neck. The sun would be setting soon. It was too late in the day to attack the rebel camp in Cambridge. In fact, they never did. The British generals gave up that idea, after they saw how bravely the Yankees had fought.

* * * * *

General Howe did not return to Boston after the battle. He spent the night sleeping on a pile of hay on Breed's Hill. He was awakened in the night by a captain who was supervising one of the burial crews. Thirty rebels had been killed inside the fort, and the captain thought the general would want to identify one of them.

"Sir, someone said the body might be the rebel Doctor Joseph Warren."

"Where is it?" Howe demanded, trying not to let his excitement show in his voice.

"I will gladly take you to it, sir," the captain answered. "We stuffed the scoundrel with another rebel into one hole. There he and his rebel ideas may remain."

They walked to the grave. General Howe could not believe his good fortune. He looked at Doctor Warren's body in the pit and said his thoughts out loud. "The greatest rebel in all of America is dead. His death is worth five hundred men to me."

CHAPTER TWENTY-TWO

Boston, two weeks later

L ydia walked Will Pitcairn to the front door. "Goodbye, Mistress Dunham. I hope my father and I were not too much trouble for you."

Lydia answered the young man, a lieutenant now. "Thank you, Lieutenant Pitcairn. You and the major were not much trouble atall. I'll always be grateful for the major finding my Eben and bringing him home the night before the battle. And for buying the medicine to help Eben get well. He was a good man, your father."

"Yes, yes, I know, madam. A very good man. We shall all miss him terribly. ... Perhaps, under different circumstances, we could have – could have – been friends – your family and mine. Well, I'm off to my new quarters."

Will Pitcairn nodded his head and gave a half bow before walking away from the house. He had borrowed a wagon to carry his belongings and what remained of his dead father's. Most of his father's things, though, Will had already given away to the major's many friends in the army.

Will then turned back to Mrs. Dunham to offer one final thought before she closed the door. "And madam – I, uh, I want to thank you for one other thing."

"What is that, lieutenant?" Lydia asked.

"For – for coming to the funeral at Christ's Church that morning two weeks ago, you and your son."

She smiled. "That was my son's doing. Eben insisted we attend the major's funeral."

Will Pitcairn thought about that for a moment. "I'm sorry, madam, I did not greet you and your son in church that day, and make you both feel welcome there. The battle, you see, it was all too fresh in my mind. I did not feel like seeing any reb– uh, Americans – at my father's funeral. Surely, you can understand that, madam?"

"Yes, I understand," she said with a smile and a nod of her head.

"Well, I just want you to know that I was wrong to feel that way. I know now that you and Eben were honoring my father and paying respect to him by being there. And I thank you for that. ... Well, g'day then."

"Goodbye lieutenant, and Godspeed." Lydia Dunham went back in the house.

* * * * *

The Patriot army camp, Cambridge

"Quite a show, eh son?" Joseph Reed said, placing his arm gently around Danny's shoulders. Danny had been impressed with the ceremony. The tall, smartly uniformed Virginian – a man named George Washington – had just been given command of the whole Patriot army by the Massachusetts general, Artemas Ward. From what people in camp were saying, it was going to be a truly continental army soon. That is, just as soon as the new recruits arrive from the other colonies, the ones outside New England.

"Yes, I guess so, Father," Danny answered. "Quite a show."

Joseph Reed turned serious. "Son, I've been thinking about something a lot lately, even more so after the battle two weeks ago. I've decided I'm going to sign on again, when my enlistment expires. We need battle tested soldiers and officers to stay in the army. We'll have to fight more battles, and we'll have to start winning them, if we're going to make the British government give us our rights."

"Yes, Father. I thought you would stay on." Danny had been trying to find the time and place to tell his father his own feelings about it. Now seemed like as good a time as any, so ...

"Father, I've been thinking about it some myself, I have. If it's alright with you, sir, I don't expect I'll be staying on with you. I don't want to sign on again. I don't think I'm cut out for the soldiering life. ... Well, the truth of it is, I don't want to kill any more Redcoats. I hope you don't think I'm a coward for saying that."

His father reached out and grabbed him, pulling Danny to his chest in a bear hug. Then, letting go, he held Danny by the shoulders at arm's length and smiled at him.

"No, no, *no*, Danforth. You are *not* a coward. And don't let anyone tell you you are! You fought for the Cause, same as me, and cousin Barnabus, and Doctor Warren, and all the others. You did your part! Now it's time for you to do something just as important - go home and help Mother run the farm while I'm away. She's gonna need a man around the house."

Danny let out a long sigh. "Whew!"

His father laughed and offered a hand. "Deal?"

Danny smiled and answered. "Deal!" He grabbed hold of the hand and shook it in a strong, firm handshake, a man to man handshake.

CHAPTER TWENTY-THREE

Boston, two months later

"Whoa!" Major Moncrieff of the Royal Engineers pulled back on the reins. The wagon's horses came to a halt in front of the prison. He stepped down from the wagon, dusted off his scarlet red coat, and walked up to the prison. It was Boston's city jail, the word "GAOL" painted above the heavy double doors. Before entering, the major stopped on the steps a moment to draw in one last breath of fresh air. Then he walked through the open doorway.

"Well, if it isn't Major Moncrieff, himself." The sarcastic welcome came from William Cunningham. This dirty, unshaven man was in charge of Americans the British held as prisoners of war. "What brings you back to this Godforsaken place on such a hot August day?"

"G'day, Cunningham. I have orders here ..." the major started to answer, as he unrolled a sheet of paper. "They're for the release of a few of those rebels who were taken at Breed's Hill last June seventeenth."

"What!" Cunningham stood up. "Lemme see that!" He snatched the paper out of the major's hand. "Hmmh," he muttered as he quickly read it. "Exchanged for six captured Regulars." Cunningham lifted his head to look at the major.

"I don't like the looks of this, don't like it a bit. Those rebels, I tell you, they don't deserve to be set free! And you know it! They should stay here till they rot!"

Major Moncrieff's nose twitched. "It smells like they already have. You must take good care of them," he added sarcastically. "How many of the 30 we brought here the day after the battle are still alive?"

Cunningham thought about it for a moment before answering. "Eleven ... no, ten. They don't last long, rebels. Too weak for prison life. They drop like flies from one thing or another. Rest assured, major, they're getting what they deserve, the Yankee scum, for rebelling against their king. Rebels! – That's what they are!"

"Cunningham, just show me the six men on this list. I'll sign them out and cart them over to Boston Neck for the exchange. I don't want to spend all day in this stinkhole talking to the likes of you."

Cunningham snarled, then unlocked the door leading to the first floor cells. The first floor was for criminals and suspects, the second floor for prisoners of war. "The rebels are upstairs. Stairs are in back. Follow me, major."

They started walking down the long center hallway, cells on both sides of them. "Wait, Cunningham, what are these two Regulars doing locked up? I thought they worked for you."

Cunningham turned back and spat on the floor in front of

the cell, then pointed his cane through the iron bars at the two British Regulars inside it.

"Sergeant Neal and Corporal Royal here are doing some time for not following my orders. They thought they could take things into their own hands when I was away yesterday. But I caught them when I returned earlier than they expected me back. They were giving the rebels extra fresh air and water, against my orders."

Sergeant Neal appealed to Major Moncrieff. "They was suffocating from the heat, sir. We don't deserve –"

Bang! Cunningham's cane slammed against the iron bars. "Shaddap!" he snapped at the man inside the cell. "I'll deal with you later, for talking out of turn. Curse them rebels! If they are dead and rotting, my orders for you are the same as always – keep those windows closed!"

He led the major to the stairway. As they climbed the stairs, the stench grew worse. Major Moncrieff pulled out his silk handkerchief and held it closely over his mouth and nose.

Cunningham muttered to himself, "Insubordinate swine! *I* run this prison, and *I'll* decide how to handle rebels. A pail of water, and an hour open windows, every day. It's more than they deserve."

After his eyes got used to the darkness, Major Moncrieff looked at the prisoners. Then he took his handkerchief away from his mouth, so he could speak.

"Cunningham, you're despicable, you know that? I have a mind to report you to headquarters. Look at these poor wretches! They're filthy, and nothing but skin and bones. They look like they haven't eaten in weeks. You and that commissioner of yours must be making yourselves quite a handsome living selling the prisoners' rations."

Cunningham was not scared by Moncrieff's threat. He leaned close to the major's face and whispered with foul breath.

"If you're smart, Moncrieff, you'll mind your own business. I've got friends in high places, y'know, and so does the Commissioner of Prisoners. General Howe gave us both a free hand to do as we see fit here. As for these rebels, they can eat the heads off the nails, and gnaw on the boards, and be happy they're still alive!"

Outside, the major felt less dizzy after taking a few deep breaths of fresh air. Cunningham refused to lend him a hand putting the prisoners in the wagon. Moncrieff hadn't thought of this ahead of time, and now wished he'd brought his own servant along. He had to lift one of the prisoners, a man named Barnabus Dunham, into the wagon. But, after more than two months of starvation rations, the man was light enough.

Barnabus Dunham held up a bony arm to shield his eyes from the blinding sun. He was in a daze, and could not understand what was happening. Finally, as he was riding through Boston's streets, he muttered to himself, "My prayers have been answered. Praise and thank the Lord."

Major Moncrieff brought the wagon to a halt after going through the Town Gates on Boston Neck. Two American officers, with their own prisoners – the six British Regulars to be exchanged – were already there waiting. A few British officers were there, too. Moncrieff nodded to the British officers, and introduced himself to the two American officers, then he led them all over to his wagon.

The American officers asked the prisoners several questions about their identity and their health, then had them climb down and walk around. Barnabus had a difficult time climbing down, because of his hip.

The hip had been shattered by a British bullet on that day of the battle on Breed's Hill. During the retreat at the end of that day, he had turned back to try to save Doctor Joseph Warren, still inside the fort. But Barnabus had been shot down and captured before he could reach the fort.

One of the American officers freely expressed his disgust at the bad treatment of the prisoners. Major Moncrieff and the other British officers said nothing. They were not going to waste their time arguing with rebels. The British view of these prisoners was that they were rebels, not true prisoners of war. They did not consider this a war between nations. Instead, it was just a rebellion, so American prisoners did not deserve good treatment.

The British and American officers left the wagon and walked to a nearby maple tree. There they could stand in the shade, out of the hot sun. After a lengthy discussion, they all read and signed several papers.

When they returned, they transferred the prisoners to the other wagon. All, that is, except Barnabus Dunham. Major Moncrieff explained why.

"Mister Dunham, you are not well enough to return to active duty in the rebel forces. If you are returned to your officers there, they will take one look at you and do nothing but send you home. Therefore, since you live right here in Boston, we have all agreed that we should not bother with all that folderol. I can bring you home myself, right now. Your family can begin nursing you back to health today.

"However," the major continued, "allowing a rebel to return and live here could be a risk to our army here in town. So, instead of being exchanged, you will be paroled. All you have to do is sign this parole document. It says that you agree not to fight in the rebel army again, or commit any other rebel acts such as spying."

The major handed him the parole to read. Barnabus just stared at the paper without reading it.

"Are you ready to sign? I don't have all day," asked the major impatiently.

Barnabus could not talk. Choked with emotions, he could only nod his head yes. Moncrieff dipped the quill pen in a bottle of ink and put it in Barnabus' hand.

"Sign the document, man. All three copies."

Barnabus put the papers down on the bed of the wagon and signed them, in a very shaky hand, where the British officer pointed.

Major Moncrieff took back the pen and documents. He gave one copy to an American officer, one copy to Barnabus, and kept the other copy. Turning, he shouted an order to one of the British sentries at the gate. "You there, soldier! Come over here and help this rebel back in the wagon."

Afterwards, Major Moncrieff pulled on his gloves and climbed back onto the wagon seat. Pulling on the reins and gently talking to the horses, he turned them around. The wagon slowly headed back into Boston town. The horses' hooves made rhythmic *clip-clop* sounds on the street's cobblestones.

Silent tears rolled down Barnabus Dunham's cheeks as the wagon headed towards his home on Copp's Hill.

AUTHOR'S NOTE

The Battle of Bunker Hill was important for "the Cause" – the fight for liberty. Of course, it was the first big battle of the American Revolutionary War. But its real importance was how it changed people's minds. It changed the minds of both the British and the Americans.

Soon after this battle, William Howe became the top general in the entire British army. He would now be the man who must win the war for the British King. But his bad memories of Bunker Hill stayed with William Howe. So, he became much more careful.

There were times when General Howe had his chances to defeat the American army. But, instead of boldly attacking, he often waited, hoping he could force the Americans to come out and fight on open ground. This sometimes saved the American army from being destroyed. In this way, Bunker Hill had a big effect on the mind of the top British general, so it helped George Washington's army survive and continue the war.

Bunker Hill changed the minds of many Americans, too. People did not yet think of themselves as "Americans." New Yorkers were New Yorkers; Virginians were Virginians, and so on. Why should they risk their lives in a war New Englanders – the "Yankees" – had started? Many said, "Let's wait and see if those Yankees stand their ground in a battle against the British army. Maybe if they do, we'll be willing to risk our lives, too."

Some Patriots who were in the battle wrote letters about it to friends and relatives in the other colonies. The people receiving those letters brought them down to their local newspaper office and said, "Here, print this in your newspaper, so everyone here can know that the Yankees stood their ground against the British army."

In this way, thousands of people were able to read about this battle that had happened in far off Massachusetts. And people who could not read heard about it from others. Many decided to go north to help the Yankees of New England, and form a truly continental army under George Washington. The new army had soldiers in it from all the colonies on the continent. Though it would take several years, in the end America would win the war and become its own country.

* * * * *

You may be interested to know what happened to a few of the people who were in this story. Major John Pitcairn's body still lies buried in Boston, in a vault under the floor of Christ's Church. This is the church where, two months before the battle, Paul Revere asked his friend to hang two lanterns in the steeple on the night of April 18th to signal that the British were marching to Lexington.

The Reverend Abiel Leonard, chaplain of the Patriots from Connecticut, was missed by the members of his church back home in Woodstock. They wrote to General Washington, asking if their pastor could be allowed to quit the army and go home to serve his people again. George Washington wrote back to them, saying that Reverend Leonard may be needed by his town, but he's needed even more by his country. He stayed in the army.

Besides Bunker Hill, Colonel John Stark served well in other battles, too. Two years later, he again left his wife Molly and his New Hampshire home, this time to go to the western border of Vermont and fight another British army.

There, Stark led an army of New Hampshire, Vermont, and western Massachusetts Patriots (including some Indians from Stockbridge, Mass.), in a great victory at the Battle of Bennington. Stark was determined to fight to the death, if need be. Just before he led the charge, Stark told his troops, "There are your enemies! They will be ours today, or Molly Stark sleeps a widow tonight!" This is what my other story for young people, *Gone to Meet the British*, is about; Danny and Eben are in that story, too.

In the Bunker Hill battle, Captain Thomas Knowlton led the Connecticut Patriots at the rail fence. The next year, George Washington asked him to form a special unit to do dangerous missions. They became known as "Knowlton's Rangers." Thomas Knowlton was shot and killed while rallying his Rangers during the Battle of Harlem Heights, in what is today a part of New York City.

One of Knowlton's Rangers, a young man named Nathan Hale, was caught by the British in New York, in 1776. While searching his clothes, they found drawings of the British camp. They hung Nathan Hale as a spy. Just before they did, they asked him if he had any last words. In a clear, strong voice, Nathan Hale told the crowd that came to watch the hanging, "I only regret that I have but one life to lose for my country."

For many months after the Battle of Bunker Hill, the Americans wondered what had happened to Doctor Joseph Warren. Was he killed, or perhaps captured in the fort? Finally, after the British left Boston a year later, an American digging party went up to the top of Breed's Hill. They wanted to find the bodies that the British had buried there. They must dig them up, and rebury them properly in cemeteries.

In the skull of one skeleton they dug up, the silversmith Paul Revere saw some of his own work. Because Paul had done some dental work on Doctor Warren's teeth a few years before, he knew this skeleton must be the good doctor.

By staying to the end, Joseph Warren covered the retreat of his fellow Patriots escaping out the narrow opening in the back wall of the fort. He gave his life so that others might live. Joseph Warren was a great leader. Many people thought, if he had lived, he might have one day become president of the new nation.

I hope you enjoyed reading this story; I enjoyed writing it.

One final note – I'd like to thank Todd Gerlander for his excellent illustrations, Ron Godbey for his cover photo and computer assistance, and Andrew Guerette for posing as Danforth Reed. And thank you, as well, to Mr. Tom Ferriter for allowing us to photograph on his property.

Gregory T. Edgar
Somers, CT

GLOSSARY

Artillery. All types of cannons.

Bayonet. A 17 inch long, three sided blade a soldier put on the end of his musket.

Boston Neck. In 1775, Boston was a peninsula connected to the mainland by a narrow strip of land. On a map, it looked like a neck connecting a head to a body. So the people called this narrow strip of land "Boston Neck." Charlestown Neck connected Charlestown to the mainland.

Breastwork. A wall, usually made of earth. It was about as high as a man's chest, or breast. It was thrown up very quickly, for defense against an enemy about to attack.

Captain. In an army, a captain is the officer in charge of a company (see "Company," below). In a navy, a captain is in charge of the whole ship.

Cartridge. A musket ball and enough gunpowder to fire it, wrapped together in paper. Up to 60 cartridges could fit in a "cartridge box," which was a leather case. It had a leather strap to sling over your shoulder so the case could rest on your hip.

Cat-o'-nine-tails. The "cat" was a whip used for "flogging" (whipping). This was a very common form of punishment in armies in those days. The cat was made of nine leather cords attached to a handle. If a soldier did something wrong, an officer would order an adult drummer to whip that soldier with the cat-o'-nine-tails.

Colonel. (pronounced "ker-nel") The officer in charge of a "regiment." A regiment had about ten companies of soldiers.

Common. A New England village had its church and many houses close together around the village green. The people called this grassy area "the common" because it was a shared place for all the village's animals to graze.

Company. A unit of soldiers in an army, led by a captain. It had at least 40 musketmen, plus several lower officers (lieutenants, sergeants and corporals) and a drummer. American companies and British grenadier companies also had a fifer.

In an American company, most of the soldiers would be from the same village. They would vote for who they wanted to be their captain. The captain would then choose his lower officers.

However, in the British army it was much different. There, the captain would buy his position from the colonel.

Cupola. A tiny, square room built in the middle of a house's roof. In seaport towns, such as Boston, people living in such houses could look out from their cupola and see the ships coming into the harbor.

Fishmonger. Someone who often came into town to sell freshly caught fish. He would sell the fish in a two-wheeled cart he pushed through the streets, yelling, "Fish! Fish!"

Flank Attack. In a flank attack, one force attacks a line of soldiers from the side (flank). If the bullet missed the target (the first soldier in the line) it would continue along and probably hit some other soldier further down the line. Because of this, you never wanted to let your enemy flank you (attack you from the side).

General. An officer higher than a colonel.

Grenadiers. A company of British soldiers specially selected because they were big and strong. Often they were picked to lead the charge, to put fear in the enemy.

Huzzah! Just before they charged, soldiers would all shout one loud "Huzzah!" This gave them courage and put fear in their enemy. If they won the battle, afterwards they would shout "Huzzah!" three times to celebrate the victory.

Knee britches. In 1775, men and boys wore trousers that only came down a little below their knees, and long stockings that came above the knees.

Laudanum. A pain killing medicine made from opium and alcohol.

Lieutenant. An officer in charge of a platoon, which was half a company.

Major. An officer lower than a colonel, but higher than a captain. A major might be in charge of four or five companies. Each company had a captain.

Muster Day. During peacetime, once a month the Patriots in a village would gather on the village "common," or green, and practice marching and loading their muskets on muster day.

Outhouse. (also called a "little house," a "privy," or a "necessary") A small wooden outdoor shelter in the backyard, or in the woodshed. Inside was a seat, and below that a hole in the ground. If the outhouse had two seats – and two doors – the door with a round sun carved on it was for males, and the door with a crescent moon carved on it was for females.

Paces. Colonel Stark pounded his wooden stake in the sand on the Mystic River beach after walking off forty "paces" in front of the stone wall. A pace was the distance covered by a normal marching step, which was about two and a half feet.

Parole. A paper signed by a prisoner when released from prison. It stated certain conditions that the parolee (the released prisoner) must promise to obey, such as not fighting again, and staying in town. If the parolee broke any of these conditions, he would be returned to prison.

Patriots. Americans who didn't like some of the laws of the British government. The British called the Patriots "rebels" because they were rebelling against their king.

Quarters. A house or other place where someone in an army lives.

Ramrod. A rod (usually metal, though riflemen liked to use a hard wood) used for ramming a ball or cartridge down the barrel of a rifle or musket.

Rank. A row of soldiers.

Rations. A daily ration was how much food each soldier was allowed. A soldier's wife, sweetheart, or child, if enrolled in the army as a "camp follower," was usually given rations equal to about half as much.

Rebels. See "Patriots," above.

Regulars. The soldiers of a nation's professional army. For example, the British soldiers were Regulars, the American Patriots at first were irregulars. But once the Continental army was formed (after Bunker Hill) under George Washington, its soldiers would be called Regulars, too.

Sentries. Soldiers on guard duty or watch duty.

Teched in the head. An expression that meant someone was crazy, insane.

Tories. Loyalists. Americans who were for the British government and against the Patriots. The Patriots felt that the Tories were traitors and should be hung, but that almost never happened. A Patriot joke back then went like this: "A Tory is someone whose head is in England, and whose body is in America, and whose neck needs to be stretched." About one third of all Americans were Tories, another third were Patriots, and the final third tried to not take sides.

Volley. A group of soldiers all firing at the same time was called firing off a "volley."

Yankees. In 1775, a "Yankee" was someone from New England. The word "yankee" came from the way some of the Indians in the early 1600s tried to pronounce the word "English" – they would say "yeng-gees."

"CANNON BALLS"

(Tune: "Jingle Bells")

1. The Yankees soon will learn, the news we Redcoats bring,
That cannon balls and musket balls, soon in the air will sing.
Our uniforms do shine, making our march grand,
Oh what fun it will be, to conquer this great land.

Oh, ... cannon balls, cannon balls, shot off by the ton,
Oh what fun it will be, to see those Yankees ru-un.
Cannon balls, cannon balls, shot off by the ton,
Oh what fun it will be, to see those Yankees run.

Boom, boom, boom, boom. Boom, boom, boom, boom.

2. Our planned surprise attack, the rebel spies found out,
So up Breed's Hill they went, dirt flying all about.
The rebels dug all night, to beat us to the punch,
We could have come this morn, but stopped to have our
lunch.

Oh, ... cannon balls, cannon balls, shot off by the ton,
Oh what fun it will be, to see those Yankees ru-un.
Cannon balls, cannon balls, shot off by the ton,
Oh what fun it will be, to see those Yankees run.

Boom, boom, boom, boom. Boom, boom, boom, boom.

3. From Britain we have come, to meet New England's best,
Now up the hill we march, to put them to the test.
Behind their walls they hide, they don't fight fair in battle,
With bay-o-nets we'll charge, and make them all skedaddle!

Oh, ... cannon balls, cannon balls, shot off by the ton,
Oh what fun it will be, to see those Yankees ru-un.
Cannon balls, cannon balls, shot off by the ton,
Oh what fun it will be, to see those Yankees run!!

PRAISE FOR GONE TO MEET THE BRITISH

"Edgar has captured well the flavor of the times with his characters, both American and British."
- Clavin Fisher, author of <u>A Spy at Ticonderoga</u> and <u>Three Spies for General Washington</u>

"<u>Gone to Meet the British</u> is an excellent way to present this period of America's history."
- David Garland, author of <u>Saratoga</u>

"<u>Patriots</u> and <u>Gone to Meet the British</u> should be in every school library. Edgar has a knack for reaching young Americans, bringing our history to life as the vivid story that it is."
- Dave Palmer, History Channel consultant, author of <u>George Washington & Benedict Arnold</u>

"Edgar's readers feel what it was like to be a youth in the War for Independence."
- James F. Morrison, author of <u>The Forgotten Livingston: Colonel James Livingston</u>

"A refreshing book that entertains and enlightens as its story unfolds, helping students understand a time and place different from their own. The main characters provide a bridge to introduce historical personalities like Benedict Arnold and the Green Mountain Boys, and make them come alive. Excellent."
- Leo West, book critic, *News & Views*, PA Council for Social Studies

"<u>Gone to Meet the British</u> is an engaging novel based on real-life historical events. The dialect is accurate for the time. Mr. Gerlander's ten illustrations enhance the book."
- Curtis Wong, *Hartford Courant*

"Mr. Edgar is truly gifted in bringing history to life for young adults. <u>Gone to Meet the British</u> is every bit as enlightening as his

first book. The Teacher Guides are also beneficial. A+ rating."
 - Shelley Ashcroft, book critic, *Homeschool Exchange* magazine

"Both young and old will enjoy meeting Danny, Eben and Molly, and seeing how young people can overcome political and cultural differences and learn to be friends."
 - Julie Turner, With Pipe & Book bookstore, Lake Placid, NY

"Few books tell the story from the viewpoint of the young, sometimes confused and frightened soldier who actually fought this war. I consider <u>Gone to Meet the British</u> *excellent, and heartily recommend it."*
 - David Bernier, Major General, Living History Association

Other Books by Gregory T. Edgar

To purchase **Gone to Meet the British,** please contact BluewaterPress, LLC at bluewaterpress.com.

. **Gone to Meet the British** (free Teacher's Guide available upon request). This is the sequel to **Patriots.** Two years after Bunker Hill, Danny Reed and Eben Dunham are recruited to go west and reinforce the American northern army. This army is trying to stop a British army from Canada that is invading Vermont and New York's Hudson River Valley.

Danny is still tormented by traumatic memories of Bunker Hill. But he goes along to try to prevent his cousin Eben from suffering the same. Danny's personal torment is complicated further by a sudden romantic interest in Molly Cameron, a lost British camp follower the boys meet in the woods near Bennington, VT. Molly must pose as a rebel until they can find a way for her to rejoin her father, a soldier in the British army.

Though they start out as enemies, Danny and Molly soon find they are attracted to each other. Their personal fate, and that of American liberty, both hang in the balance, as two mighty armies clash on the battlefield near Saratoga, NY. There, Danny and Eben will come face to face with Molly's father.

Non-fiction Books (adult reading level):

. **"Liberty or Death!" The Northern Campaigns in the American Revolutionary War.** This book, nominated for the Society of the Cincinnati's Cincinnati Prize for a distinguished book on the Revolutionary Era, follows the northern department of the Continental army, and the armies that opposed it. In the fall of 1775, the Patriots boldly march north, in an unsuccessful attempt to seize Canada from Britain. The British strike back in both 1776 and 1777, heading southward from Canada, aiming to reach the Hudson River and isolate New England from the other colonies. The British are finally stopped at the decisive battles of Saratoga, the turning point of the war. Colorful characters include the fiery Patriot leaders Ethan Allen, Benedict Arnold and Daniel Morgan, the flamboyant British commander "Gentleman Johnny" Burgoyne, the beautiful martyr Jane McCrae, and "Mrs. General" – the Baroness Fredericka von Riedesel.

. **Campaign of 1776, The Road to Trenton.** This book, nominated for the Fraunces Tavern Museum Book Award, covers the political and military movements in the pivotal year 1776.

George Washington must somehow turn a "rabble in arms" into an army capable of opposing a powerful British army and navy, commanded by two brothers, General William Howe and Admiral Richard Howe. After a series of crushing victories, the Howes are on the verge of ending the war, when George Washington suddenly turns the tables. On Christmas night, facing the imminent dissolution of his army, and perhaps with it the Revolution itself, he risks all in a surprise attack at Trenton. Included are stories of the spy Nathan Hale, and David Bushnell's "famous water machine" – the world's first submarine.

. **Reluctant Break with Britain, From Stamp Act to Bunker Hill.** Repeated attempts at compromise fail to prevent the outbreak of war between the mother country and her thirteen colonies. Relive the Boston "massacre" and the Sons of Liberty's riotous "tea party." Judge for yourself who fired the "shot heard 'round the world" on Lexington Common that fateful morning of April 19, 1775, after you read the personal accounts of participants on both sides. The book concludes with a rousing, detailed presentation of the misnamed Battle of Bunker Hill, the first major battle of the Revolutionary War.

. **The Philadelphia Campaign 1777-1778.** Washington fights Howe for the capital city, then his own subordinates who conspire to replace him at Valley Forge. Lafayette, the teenage French general, supports him. Drilled into an effective army by the Prussian, von Steuben, the Patriots at last are able to stand their ground and match their foes at the controversial Battle of Monmouth. Included is a colorful account of the *Mischianza*, a social extravaganza in British occupied Philadelphia.